OVER HILL OVER DALE

STUDENTS AND INSTRUCTORS
OF THE
2020 STORY MAKERS CLASS

HELD AT THE CUPBOARD MAKER BOOKS

ISBN: 978-1-7331837-4-1

Edited by Samantha Coons
Cover design by Kristian Beverly

Back Cover image:
"Once Upon A Magical Day Poppy, Rose and Cat..."
a fairytale shadow box by Judy Kelly

DEDICATION

To all those who dream through the light and the dark

Kelly

I was part of the class at Cupboard Makers Bookstore in 2020. I am still waiting for Keystone's publication that I coordinated until I retired in 2020. They are having funding issues.

please note that the story I wrote on pg 69 is the only fictional story I have ever written.

Hope you enjoy it!!

Currently I am working on creating my own book of poetry, reflections and personal stories.

Kathy ann

CONTENTS

ACKNOWLEDGMENTS

Thank you to all of the Story Makers 2020 students for their patience during these difficult times.

Special thank you from the editor to those who submitted to the anthology, for bearing with her during this process and responding so graciously to her nitpicky feedback.

So much love and appreciation to the instructors for their flexibility in hard times and excellent lessons.

Lastly, thank you to the bookstore cats for limiting their interruptions to only once or twice a class.

Negotiations Between Equals

Odessa Moon

Melantha gritted her teeth as she studied the phosphorescent swamp opening up before her. The thick, dark fir trees she had been forcing her way through had concealed it until it was too late to go in any other direction. The whisper of a breeze had been from the wrong direction, so her nose couldn't warn her until it was too late to turn back. She could no longer backtrack, not with what was dogging her heels.

That damned beast had managed to lie to her about the best path through the forest. He was not, despite what she had been promised, completely under her control. He kept proving it as well as proving he wasn't a mere dumb animal. That was something else she hadn't been told and it bothered her. What else had she not been told?

The vast swamp glowed iridescent under the full moon like scaly, newly dead fish. The mangrove trees growing up through the water were draped with fluorescent moss shining with stomach-churning shades of rot and decay. The fetid smell rising from its murky surface was strong enough to penetrate the myriad other, offensive odors hanging around her, touches of mildew and sewers and offal. Melantha stank from days on the trail but this odor made her smell fresh and perfumed with violets. Even the smells her traveling companion generated were dainty compared to this. She had thought her nose was dead to any more insults but alas, she was wrong.

The surface of the water, if you could call it that, was a shiny deep purple-gray dotted with oddly colored splotches and strewn with green and yellow waterweeds. The splotches were strange.

Were they really water? Melantha had wandered through much of the world but she had never seen water do this before. Could water sit on top of water? Still worse, it was impossible to tell how deep the swamp was or what she would be stepping on or in. Despite how offensive the swamp was, a wide variety of noxious creatures called it home.

She would have to cross. They could not backtrack through the firs. Worse, the trail they had left hacking their way through would be easy to follow with the full moon beaming down.

Melantha glanced back over her shoulder at the unicorn. He was glorious; a glowing, pearlescent treat for the eyes with a flowing golden mane and tail, silvery hooves and coat and deep amethyst eyes. He flared his nostrils at her in gleeful contempt and deliberately added to the overwhelming smell with a long, drawn out expulsion of noxious gas strong enough to make his tail flutter. Gods above and below, how she hated that snobby, supercilious beast.

To add to her irritation, her stomach growled, reminding her that it had been a long time since she had eaten anything other than travel bread and her supplies were running low. But the unicorn now. There was a thought. It would be such a pleasure to slaughter the wretched beast, gut him, skin him, roast him and eat him. Her mouth watered at the thought of a good steak, still bloody in the middle with that delicious charred crust, a heavy sprinkle of salt and a layer of crushed pepper to enhance the juicy, meaty, dripping succulence.

She let herself enjoy the thought as that was all the enjoyment she would get from that damned beast. He probably wouldn't taste very good as she wasn't much of a cook, but he would be food. Regrettably, she needed to get him alive to the court of Krimmin to fulfill her contract.

Riverfall yanked at the golden bridle, trying to tug it loose from her hand. It allowed *her* to control him, within certain limited definitions of control, and he hated it even more than he hated *her*. No one had ever captured him like *she* had. It was deeply humiliating to be at the beck and call of this so-called fairy maiden.

2

His only pleasure lay in finding the limits of those controls. It hadn't taken the unicorn very long to realize he could lie by omission and misdirection. *She* had been too stupid to carefully word her questions about the territory and so here they were, alongside the nastiest swamp he had ever seen. It wasn't where *she* wanted to drag him and that made it acceptable.

Melantha turned back to the disgusting murky water waiting for her, ignoring the wretched beast stamping his hooves and spraying mud everywhere. It had been a long, long time since she had last waded through anything other than a perfumed bathing pool. Normally, she would fly over and avoid the issue but that was no longer possible.

She stared at the sludgy water, hesitating. She couldn't remember how to tell if water was too deep to wade through. Did the shiny, oily patches of color mean it was safe to walk there or did they conceal poisonous traps? Were the greenish patches of weeds safe to walk on or would they entwine themselves around her legs, dragging her into the water and drowning her so she could be eaten by the various things that lived in the muck? Were they poisonous to the touch? The chittering of insects and strange calls of unseen birds told her nothing useful.

One of the dozens of annoying pixies buzzing around them dive-bombed at her, trying for a quick bite of blood and flesh. They had teeth like needles. She slapped at it and for a wonder, connected hard enough to break its spine but not kill it. The pixie fell to the ground swearing like a sailor, its shrill voice adding extra annoyance to its obscenities. It took a real effort of will for Melantha to keep from stamping on it and killing it.

The swamp pixies were vicious, bloodthirsty, and liked their meat very, very fresh. As in still alive. They *looked* like they were her miniature relatives - wings, tiny bodies proportioned like a human, and arguably capable of carrying on a conversation as if they were intelligent, sociable, civilized beings.

Pixies were nothing of the sort. They were violent, anti-social loners. They would devour their own relatives if given a chance and what little civilization they had could be defined as eat or be eaten.

Melantha spared a smile at the pixie writhing on the ground, struggling to fight off the other pixies drawn by the smell of fresh, living blood. Since it was still alive, it would be eaten to the bone within short order and that might mean that the local pixies would be full enough to leave her alone.

Pixies never ate anything dead unless they were starving.

"Surprise. You did something useful."

She started. Riverfall rarely spoke to her without being ordered to do so.

"Thank you," she answered. "And here I thought you disapproved of killing other living creatures."

The unicorn snorted, shook his heavy mane and swished his tail, trying to bat away the midges and an ambitious pixie trying for a bite of his hindquarter. "Those creatures are disgusting."

"And they'd eat you to the bone if they could."

"Amazing. You are correct about something," the unicorn replied.

Riverfall kicked at another pixie and connected, throwing it to the ground with broken wings and, from its shrill screams, other broken things as well. Even before it hit the ground, more pixies swarmed its tiny body, and began tearing off bites.

Melantha spat into the water, clarifying the muck for an instant. They were disgusting cannibals and it was impossible they were related to her species in any way.

She stared back over at the murky swamp. She did not want to think about what she'd be stepping on or in as she and Riverfall waded through to the far side. She also wasn't clear on how far away the distant shore was. The dim light of the swamp gave no clues and the moss-draped trees concealed the far shore. As she peered through the mists, trees seemed to move. She hoped it wasn't too far. She had only a day's worth of travel bread and water left in her pack. The detour Riverfall had sent her on had wasted days and caught the attention of bandits. The water lapping at the shore looked guaranteed to provide dysentery or the bloody flux at best and a messy, agonizing death at worst.

She looked back at the unicorn, staring around him at the mossy trees and weedy undergrowth with disdain, whisking his tail and twitching his skin madly to keep off pixies. It was worth a try.

"We have to cross the swamp. We could make better time if you let me ride you."

The unicorn looked even more disgusted.

"As if I would allow a dissipated creature like you on my back. You are not a virgin and you haven't been one for a long, long time. And you are my captor. Let us not forget that."

"You are such a snob, you know that? I'm not a virgin. So what." Melantha smirked at the unicorn's disapproval. "Men are enormous fun when they try. And don't you try and tell me you're a virgin. Unicorns breed just like horses do. I've watched. You weren't gelded as a foal."

"That's different."

"Uh-huh."

Riverfall stepped to the water's edge and cautiously put in a hoof. The murky water closed around his hoof, swallowing the soft glow of his pure silvery white fur and hoof. He pulled it back out, shaking off the oozy brown liquid, making sure to spatter her clothes still further. Not a drop landed on his coat, staining its velvety perfection.

"This is disgusting. If I have to wade through this cesspool, so do you."

Riverfall tossed his mane and added in a silky voice, "You could fly above it, you know. You do have wings."

Melantha did have wings and under normal circumstances she would fly over the swamp, never letting any part of her body touch its nastiness. But these were not normal circumstances and she was unable to fly. She hoped to change that situation and the sooner the better.

"Thanks for reminding me. Let me tighten up that bridle."

He jerked back, but the golden bridle allowed Melantha to control him. He had to do her bidding, within certain limits that she kept discovering the hard way, but he had no freedom until she gave it to him of her own free will.

5

Sadly, one of the limits was that being a unicorn, Riverfall didn't have to allow any non-virgin on his back. It was part of his innate magic, just like the soft, silvery glow surrounding him at all times. The glow was both useful, as it made it easier to see, and a real hindrance when trying to travel without being seen by someone else. Anyone with eyes could spot a unicorn, day or night and in any weather.

"Fine," she said. "We'll both wade."

A hunting horn sounded far away, the sound just audible over the buzzing cloud of pixies devouring their fallen comrades. The calling birds immediately fell silent.

"Shit," Melantha said. "Shit and double shit. I thought we'd lost them. Let's get moving."

She quit hesitating and carefully waded out into the swamp, Riverfall compelled by the bridle to follow. He high-stepped like a parade horse, shaking each hoof clean before dropping it back into the murk. It seemed like he aimed each spray of muddy water at her clothes, adding to their dirty raggedness.

Perhaps not, she thought. They needed to move fast. He knew as well as she did what followed them.

As they waded through the fetid water, more pixies showed up, hovering about and trying for a bite of flesh. Melantha batted at them and Riverfall swished his tail and kicked, both trying for the non-fatal injuries that would draw their cannibalistic brethren in for the kill and distract them from the fugitives.

They had to keep moving, despite what lay beneath sucking at their feet, and what flitted about their heads. The hunters following them were far more dangerous to Melantha than whatever lurked in the fetid water surrounding her.

"Those bandits could still catch us, you know," Riverfall said urbanely, as if he was commenting on the weather. "I'd get to watch you get your wings torn off and suffer the worst kind of torment until you beg for death. Then I'd be free."

Melantha spared a contemptuous look back at him. "Free. You really believe that? Well, you are a type of horse so I shouldn't be surprised at that level of stupidity."

Deeply offended, he jerked his head, trying to pull the bridle loose. It didn't do any good and he knew it, but he kept trying.

"Those thugs would chop off your horn, slaughter you, and eat you. Your horn will bring a huge price, along with your hooves, hide, bones, mane and tail, plus eating you would give them a permanent boost to their virility."

She laughed suddenly, a silvery ripple of pleasure. It was the first real amusement she'd had in days.

"Why, I'd get to watch them slaughter you and eat you first, before they started on me. They'd last longer then, you know?"

Riverfall snorted, letting all of his inborn prudishness show. "And you voluntarily lie with men."

"Men I choose, not goons like them. There is a difference."

"Just like there is a difference between unicorns and horses. I am not a horse."

"True, true. If you were just another horse, neither of us would be here."

The horn sounded again, just a bit louder.

Melantha said, trying not to sound too hopeful, "Are you sure I can't ride you? We'd make better time." She was proud of herself for not letting her desperation show. That would give Riverfall an element of control over her, one he would take full advantage of.

The horn sounded again, much closer. Worse, a hoarse voice called out, "I see them! The unicorn and the fairy slut! Come on, lads! Good fun, good eating, and good money are waiting."

Riverfall flicked his tail, his amythest eyes suddenly much wider. "Scramble up. I hope you can ride?"

"Horses, yes. A unicorn never."

"Why am I not surprised."

She leaped up, intensely grateful to have her feet out of the murk. To her immense relief and surprise, she did not immediately slide off to land face first in the muddy, phosphorescent water. She hadn't quite believed Riverfall would allow her on his back, especially since she was now dripping reeking mud down his flanks.

"Thank you," she said.

"You're welcome." Riverfall began trotting, his gait smooth and effortless. Melantha enjoyed the view of the swamp from her perch, high and out of the smelly muddy water.

They rode along in silence for a few moments, hearing the hunting horns grow louder as more joined the chorus and then fell silent. Melantha listened closely, hearing angry male voices at the shore. The bandits cursed the swampy water, the view of Riverfall's backside, and the buzzing, biting pixies dive-bombing this wonderful new source of meat.

"I will allow you to ride me to the other side of this swamp," Riverfall said.

"I am deeply grateful," Melantha said truthfully.

"I will throw you off my back at the other side."

"I will dismount on my own the moment you ask, even if we are still wading through this filthy water as long as I can make it to shore," Melantha conceded. She'd much rather not land on her ass or worse, face-first in the swamp.

Riverfall remained silent as they glided through the swamp, putting distance between them and the shouting, angry bandits. She didn't think he would answer. He would joyously throw her into the fetid liquid, just to watch her struggle. It wouldn't make her lose control of the golden bridle, but she'd be miserable; filthy and possibly diseased from whatever lived in the swamp. Leeches, bloodworms, tiny biting crabs, noxious lakeweeds that burned the skin on contact. All of which were surrounding Riverfall's legs with every step. She slapped at pixies, slapping them away from him as well as her.

"I will ask, but only once."

"To show my gratitude, I will scrub your legs and lower body clean of the swamp waters," Melantha said. "But I must be honest, Riverfall. I cannot free you. I have sworn to deliver you to the court of Krimmin."

"Your wings?"

"Yes, among other things."

"It's a long way to Krimmin," Riverfall replied after Melantha decided he wouldn't speak again until they reached the far shore. "Much can happen during the journey."

The shouting behind them had died down, but a shift in the wind brought the bandit's threats and hunting horns back to life.

"They're still on our tail," Melantha said. "Even so, I will not ask you to carry me past the swamp."

"Much can happen during our journey, Melantha," the unicorn repeated.

AUTHOR NOTE

This story is based on a Mimi Jobe collectable plate called 'Trails of Starlight'. I saw the image in a Sunday supermarket supplement over twenty years ago and was never able to get it out of my mind. It was so weird.

Why was a winged fairy trudging through a swamp at night? She has wings. She could fly. But she's not flying.

Wait. She's leading a unicorn. She's ankle-deep in swamp water. This unicorn is horse-sized and horses can be ridden through swamps, particularly swamps at night. But she's not riding the unicorn.

What is she doing in a swamp in the middle of the night anyway? Sensible people don't traipse around in swamps late at night. It's harder to see the alligators, poisonous snakes, panthers, strangling vines, or places where the swamp bottom drops away into a drowning hazard. Or leeches. Don't forget about bloodsucking leeches.

What could possibly compel a fairy maiden to lead a unicorn through a swamp late at night; not flying and not riding?

The other question is why is the unicorn putting up with this treatment?

And thus, a story is born. Eventually I may do more with it. Melantha is in dire straits and needs a solution. No, Riverfall will not be able to transform into a man. He's a unicorn, proud of it, and insists you keep those prurient thoughts to yourself.

AUTHOR BIOGRAPHY

Odessa Moon has at various times painted, sewed, served in the Navy, worked as a sales clerk and cashier, taken care of her family, and gardened with enthusiasm. Her house and garden are a piece of performance art: a meditation on time, change, and entropy. She reads extensively, particularly on subjects like medieval history, caste, the class struggle, colonization, and resource depletion. While growing up, she read plenty of science-fiction and fantasy and wondered what the authors hand-waved away about how difficult it really would be to terraform another planet. She also read plenty of romance and wondered where the characters' relatives were and how they paid the bills. Her series The Steppes of Mars is her attempt to combine all those interests.

When Ms. Moon is not writing, she improves the soil in her own garden and plants trees in her municipality. She recommends you do the same.

Visit Odessa at Peschel Press (www.peschelpress.com) or her website, www.odessamoon.com. She can be reached at odessa@peschelpress.com.

2

A Good Deed

Nellie Batz

"You ain't want to go to the north of town."

Felice's brows furrowed together as she stared down at the old woman. She was one of the few people sitting outside. Everyone else had taken shelter as soon as the sun hit the horizon. "And why is that?"

"Is haunted, so everyone says. An old witch lives out by the bog. Steals naughty children when they wander too far.

Though one of yous, nice young man he was, already went. Guess cryin' ladies gets to him. He told them he would get their young'uns back."

Felice let out a sigh. Boy had too soft a heart. "Then *I* need to get *him* back."

"Ain't good if he isn't back now. It's worse after dark. The beastie in the water probably got him."

"Beastie? What sort of beastie?"

The old woman shrugged. "Some sort of creature that makes the air around the bog smell like hot sulfur. Probably something she summoned up. Strange things happen in that bog. Some of the men pass by and swear they hear a woman calling for help. Could be that your man fell to that trap. He's probably nothing more than food for the crows."

Felice ran her tongue along her teeth. "I'd rather see for myself if he's lost."

The woman snorted.

"This ain't like the big cities." The woman peered at Felice before giving a gap-toothed smile, teeth that weren't missing an

13

alarming shade of yellow and black. "For a handful of silver, I have a charm that will help you ward off evil."

"Well, I'm a little more prepared to deal with some beastie or strange woman in the water than your lost children. I think I'll be fine. I won't need a charm." She's seen a lot of creatures at sea. Some bog beast was the least of her worries.

"That will be your mistake."

Tommy was going to be bait for a leviathan when Felice caught up with him. She made a face as she took a step into the bog, the mud sucking on her boots. It was the third time she wound up barefooted.

"If he's lucky, he'll be dead before I get ahold of him."

The crone hadn't been kidding when she said that the area smelled wrong. If she wasn't used to a shipful of men who hadn't bathed for a month, it would be enough to make her pass out before she even got close to the water. She shone a light around, the beam barely cutting through the thick fog.

"Thomas! Thomas Mender! Where are you?"

She stopped, tilting the lantern, only for it to bounce back from the mass of white clouds.

"I swear to the gods, I'm going to make you wash the deck for a month."

She scowled. The longer she was out in this mess, the more things she was going to add to the list of work for him.

In the midst of the fog, there was a splash and a horse's low nicker. She turned towards the sound and stopped, her boots squelching in the mud. If someone's work horse had wandered in as well, she would use it to make her way around the bog and save herself. Felice reached up and pushed a button on the side of her eyepatch. The gears shifted and a lens dropped down, showing the heat outline of the beast. It burned bright. Brighter than any animal should. Maybe the town used a hot blooded breed.

"Here, horse." She clicked her tongue. "I don't have any treats but help a girl out."

She saw the heated image turn and move towards her with rhythmic splashing steps. As it came closer, an acrid smell hit her nose. Hot metal and sulfur. Felice watched it, wary as it came closer. She turned off the eyepatch and saw how sickly it looked, ribs protruding. It was five feet away when she saw the twin beams of light where its eyes were, a brackish green color. It gave a hiss and lunged towards her. The forelegs shifted and became claws that latched onto her arms as its body slammed into her, shoving her down.

Felice barely had time to take a breath before the water rushed over her face. She struggled to pull the claws off her, the heat searing her skin and they locked tighter, squeezing painfully. She lashed out to punch it in the face, her hand slamming into metal. She clenched her teeth together, pushing herself not to open her mouth. She kicked at the creature's body and it landed on a part that gave. The beast bucked and needle teeth sunk onto her shoulder. The scream worked up her throat, her body overriding her brain to keep her mouth shut, the air escaped her mouth in a burst of bubbles. With a thrust, the beast went further down into the water as spots danced in Felice's eyes and her lungs screamed for air. It jerked to a stop and the claws released from her arms. Something grabbed her by the back of her vest, yanking upward. She lost consciousness, wondering if she was going to be ripped to shreds by another beast.

Wet dog. Wet dog and bog water hit her nose. Something gave a sharp compression on her chest and Felice jerked, turning to the side as vile water came rushing out of her lungs to spill onto the ground. She gave a sharp inhalation, breaking into a coughing fit, vomiting up a mixture of water and stomach bile.

"Oh, thank the gods, Captain. Marcus got you."

The soft voice pulled her attention as she turned her head, cheek resting on the ground as she pushed dark hair out of her face. She stared at the bare-chested young man with the dirty blonde hair as he crouched next to her, clutching at an arm that hung limp by his side. He gave her a tentative smile.

"You. I'm going to punch you now." She pushed herself up and gave a wild swing.

He yelped and scrambled back, falling on his ass in the mud as she was grabbed from behind, so she didn't face plant onto the ground.

"Easy, Cap'n. You can ring the boy's neck later."

"I got more than a lungful of that nasty water and now I have a beef with that beast. I've deserve to punch the person who put me in that situation."

She growled, wobbling as she turned to glare at the shaggy, wet man who was holding her upright, a shirt wrapped around his waist to cover his naked lower body. "Now let me go so I can punch Tommy and then go after that thing."

"It was a kelpie." Tommy interjected softly, flinching back when she swung her head to glare at him. "It was in one of those books from the last port. The one everyone made fun of me for getting. But it's not normal. Kelpies are flesh and blood. This one is different."

"Guess you and those odd books are coming in handy, eh? Either way, it's going to be a pile of trash when I'm done." She stumbled to her feet, hacking up a piece of plant onto the ground.

Marcus snorted and straightened her up, pulling her back. "Again, it can wait until you're in better condition."

"I'm fine. It will take more than being half drowned to keep me down." She shot a look towards him. "You smell like wet dog."

"You say it like it's an insult, Cap'n. You're bleeding. Those wounds need to be looked after. And you don't want to go into that water with open wounds. We can come back later, if you want to take it down."

Felice ground her teeth and opened her mouth to protest.

Marcus held up his hand. "That thing wasn't all flesh. My claws scratched against metal. We aren't prepared to fight whatever that is."

Her mouth shut with a snap and she glared towards the water, gave another cough and turned towards the town.

Tommy walked next to her while Marcus trailed behind, keeping watch over his shoulder. "Kids were disappearing. I thought I would help. Thought maybe they got lost in the woods. I was on the other side of the bog when I saw that thing. I thought it was a lost horse until it started to run at me and I saw sharp teeth."

"I found him up a tree, clinging to it like a baby kitten." Marcus interjected behind them.

She shot Tommy a look.

"We need to have a discussion about your urge to help the downtrodden. You're a pirate. Some would question if you follow the code or would rather be working a market stall with a wife and kids somewhere."

He looked down as he walked next to her. "I'm sorry, Captain. I didn't mean for you to get dragged into this. I can help-"

"Your arm is broken, boy. There isn't much that you'll be able to do." Marcus interrupted. "How are you going to help when you're already hobbled?"

"Umm," Tommy stuttered to a stop. "I can hold a gun with one hand."

Marcus smirked. "You'd get blown down from the kickback."

The kid grimaced and looked down. "I'm sorry, Captain. Marcus."

"We'll discuss what you can do to repay both of us for saving your hide later, Thomas. Right now, I need to figure out what to use. His claws didn't work. Though I kicked it and something gave like flesh. So it wasn't all metal. Short of pulling a cannon over by the water, we need to find something. Explosives." She mused. "Blow it up from the inside."

"Are you kicking me off the crew, Captain?" Tommy glanced at her.

Felice let out a slow breath before looking over. He looked like he had more than a bad day, clutching his upper arm to keep it still.

"I'm not kicking you out. But you really need to be careful of the tasks you take. Not everyone is going to reward you for doing what you think is good. You are still new to this. I don't know why you wanted to join, but this could have been a lot worse."

"Yeah, kid. You put your captain in danger because you wanted to be a good guy."

Tommy looked down, giving a nod. "I'm sorry."

Felice sighed before cuffing him on the shoulder. "Head to Rachet to get your arm set. I'm going to hunt this kelpie." She nodded towards Marcus. "Take him back to the ship get him patched up. Get some dynamite and a heavy hammer. Meet me back here."

"I can go after it myself, Cap'n."

"I've had worse scratches from a brawl. And no one is going alone against this thing."

He shrugged. "All right. I'll get the supplies."

"Bring back some bandages. I'll wrap myself up."

"Yes, Cap'n."

Felice paced just outside the town, waiting for Marcus. She glanced around when she heard the clearing of a throat and turned, seeing the man walk towards her, his eyes glowing when they flicked in her direction.

"Ready, Cap'n?"

"Got the dynamite?"

"Merrell almost put a bow on them. I told him that it wasn't necessary."

She smirked as they skirted along the outside of the town. "He gets a little too excited over making explosives."

The night was dead quiet. There weren't any sounds from frogs or the screams of nocturnal predators. The fog was still thick and she smelled the water before her foot sank into the mud. "I'm tired of this. Give me the sea any day."

Marcus snorted, shaking his head. "Whatever manner of abomination this is, it makes the water foul."

"Guess we learn something new every day."

"You said you kicked flesh?"

"Yes. I was told by an old woman that a witch lives on the other side and she makes creatures to guard the place. Could be this kelpie is the beastie."

He grunted. "Good to know."

"...help me...."

The breathy voice came to them from out of the fog.

Marcus stopped and turned his head, nostrils flaring before a low growl vibrated in his throat.

"What?" She turned towards the voice as it called out to them again.

"The smell."

"Hot metal and sulfur."

He looked over at her, his eyes glowing a bright yellow. "Yes."

"That's what I smelled before it jumped me. Watch yourself."

He shrugged, nostrils flaring again. "I'll be the bait."

Felice gave him a look as he called out, moving into the dense clouds.

"Hello! Young lady, where are you?"

His voice started to deepen as she could see his form bulk up and shift under the skin.

"Good sir, please come forward. I'm stuck. Please...help me. I'm so scared."

He gave a guttural snort while Felice pulled out the wrapped explosives. Merrell had been smart and rigged up a harness so it could be wrapped around a person.

The voice kept talking. Felice heard the splashing of water as the creature moved. She kept her gaze on the spot where Marcus disappeared shifting from one foot to another, letting out a slow breath. She wasn't going to let this creature grab her again. It called out, the query cut off as Felice heard the howl of the wolf followed by the mechanically reverberating squeal of a horse. Water thrashed around in the struggle.

"Marcus, I can't help if I can't see you!" Her hand tightened on the explosive while she reached up to see using her eyepatch for heat signatures. It turned on in time for her to see the large mass of red come flying at her as the kelpie squealed. She cursed and dodged out of the way as it landed, the fish tail flailing as the metal forehooves shifted to form long claws, pulling itself around to face the werewolf that came bursting out, slamming into the beast.

The huge wolf lunged at the kelpie as it lashed out, its mouth gaping open to expose needle teeth, sinking them into his shoulder. Marcus snarled as dark blood splattered on the ground.

Felice used the distraction he was giving her to leap towards the kelpie only to have the tail lash out and catch her in the stomach, flinging her back to land on the ground with a thud, driving the breath from her lungs. She wheezed and pushed herself up as it lashed out with the claws again, ripping skin along the side of

Marcus's face. His grip loosened enough for it to push him off and scramble for the water and obfuscating fog.

Marcus grabbed hold of the tail and sank his teeth into it, giving a rough shake of his head as it screeched, a shrill piercing sound. His ears pinned to his head and he clamped his jaws tighter.

Felice stumbled and covered her ears, stumbling back. She shook her head as the two creatures rolled around on the ground. Marcus lost his grip when the kelpie sunk its claws into his sides.

"FOR FUCK'S SAKE, FELICE! GET IT!" Marcus howled, clamping huge paws around the kelpie as it made another attempt to get back into the water.

She smelled burning fur and jumped towards the kelpie, wrapping the loop of rope around the neck. It thrashed and whipped its head back, slamming into her face. There was a crunch and burst of pain in her nose. Felice fell back, blinking rapidly as hot blood gushed over her lip before her hands tightened and yanked the loop before pulling off the cap, striking it on the metal of the kelpie's upper body.

"Done!"

Marcus let go of the kelpie to pluck her off its back and tossed her like a ragdoll before pushing himself away with a thrust of his hind legs.

It gave a long hiss at them, the smell of hot metal and sulfur intensifying before it leapt and dove into the water. A moment later, a large explosion caused a plume of water to explode into the air.

Felice landed with a thud and barely pushed herself up when pieces of hot metal and flesh rained down around them, her ears ringing from close proximity to the concussive force. Marcus cursed and lunged so that he was over her, taking the brunt of the falling items.

An amputated claw landed next to them, still twitching.

"How short did you make the fuse?"

"Huh?" She squinted at him, his voice muffled from the ringing in her ears. "What did you say?"

"Nevermind." He flopped to the side, skin rippling as he shifted back to his human form. "This better count as a good deed for the year. Hell, for a decade."

AUTHOR BIOGRAPHY

Nellie lives in South Central Pennsylvania, kept company by five felines of varying temperaments and a Welsh Pembrooke Corgi who is a legit drama queen. She works on chainmaille jewelry, learning how to draw and book binding.

She is a fan of all things fantasy, has a fondness for dinosaurs and considers age to be a level and is currently working on research for high level spells in preparation of the zombie apocalypse, Skynet or the Flying Spaghetti Monster.

3

Karma Karen

Kristian Beverly

Karen Mallory smoothed down the front of her blue dress before opening up the door to the very first paid visitors of Westminster Plantation. Her stomach churned with excitement. She pushed her blonde bangs out of her eyes. She loved the inverted bob haircut she'd told her hairdresser to give her. If the pesky woman had honored her coupon that'd only expired a month earlier, she'd even have left a tip.

She'd started her plan of opening up the plantation to weddings as soon as she'd finished signing the ownership paperwork. It'd been a perfect location, and she couldn't believe the deal she'd gotten. So cheap. Her life crisis purchase was coming along.

The bride and groom held out their hands for her to shake while the groomsmen and bridesmaids stood behind them. She imagined the money falling from their manicured fingers. The photographer smiled, balancing his equipment in his hands.

They wore baby blue dresses and black tuxes, minus the bride. She looked dashing in the white puffy wedding dress.

The grounds keeper, Mack, gave her a sour look before pulling his lips back from his lips and giving her a smile. An odd man, that Mack was. Along with the land, she'd inherited the groundskeeper. He'd come with raving reviews and only requested being able to leave the grounds once a year. Karen's cup ran over in luck.

They'd wanted to take photos first, and Karen had the perfect place for it. She led them down the path, past the brick kitchen, the wooden carriage house and blacksmith shop. They'd all been redone by the previous owners—a mix of giving it a modern touch while keeping the soul of original. No, what she wanted to show them had merely been swept out. Someone replaced the door and shutters but otherwise the place was still in original shape.

"See, you," she said to the bride and groom, "could stand at the door. The groomsmen and bridesmaid could each take a window. That'd look nice since there are four windows."

The bride and groom grinned—nodding their heads. "The brick would look amazing with our outfits."

Karen smiled. "I don't know what the slaves did to their living space, but it's the one place that's held up and never need refurbished."

They started towards the slave quarters.

"Maybe we could take the photo somewhere else?"

Karen paused and turned to see who'd said that. She rolled her eyes. Slavery ended so long ago and why waste such a pretty space.

That Black woman had the audacity to poke out her lips. "I just don't think we should take wedding photos in the slave quarters. It feels really disrespectful."

No one moved. Karen realized she had to smooth this over. "The people who used to live here are long gone. It's just a building and one with beautiful brick that'll offset everyone."

The Black woman looked at her before turning to the bride. "I love you both, but you already knew how I felt about it being here. I won't take photos in the slave quarters. You wouldn't have wedding photos in Dachau's sleeping areas."

Karen imagined how the Black woman would've been dealt with back in the days of this quarters' usage. The bride looked at the groom before stepping down and requesting a different spot for a photo session.

Karen's façade began to falter as she watched the party move away from her. What if in the future more of Them took issue with her photography choices? They always wanted to find something to be offended about. She'd even been inclusive in saying everyone would look good against the red brick.

Her first wedding and it wasn't the attendees who'd wanted to cry first.

Something moved in the tree line, and Karen was sure it was a person. Her whole mood no longer felt sunny and excited—but at least she held herself together to not shed a tear.

Movement near the slave quarters caught in the corner of her eyes. She'd had enough with it. Stepping into the building, she saw nothing. Just the worn, faded brick and wooden floors.

White light erupted from the blackness. Translucent faces in shapeless clothes that reminded her of burlap peered at her. Horror rose within her. What type of demented trick was this?

"Whoever is doing this should speak to me! Unacceptable!" she yelled.

Mack appeared from behind the translucent bodies. A knowing grin spread across his face before his eyes dimmed in sadness. Karen froze, ready to run.

"This has been my home for centuries. Since they took me as a boy to the auction block and I ended up here. I've watched this place be sold and bought—and I've yet to find someone who didn't want to whore it out. Those who lived and died here notice. I feel their pain. Shame others don't. These plantations are America's concentration camp."

Mack pointed his finger and the translucent bodies charged forward. Karen squeaked before clamping her eyes shut—wishing for this nightmare to end.

The noises around her cut off into silence. She opened her eyes and realized she was in the slave quarters, but red flames danced in the fireplace.

Two men clasped her wrists and dragged her out. She didn't know why it smelled so foul, why there were Black people in that awful burlap clothing, and a tall thin man with blonde hair staring at her the way one looked at a bad dog. She never planned on her plantation looking this way. No reenactments. That stuff belonged in history.

"Let go of me!" Karen yelled.

"Jus do what he's saying," the man holding her to her left said. He had a long-jagged scar that went down the side of his face. "If you make a fuss, it'll be worse. You know this Ruth."

Karen faltered. Ruth? Who was that? She looked down at her legs and her arms and noticed a difference in pigmentation.

"Make him angry and he'll just beat you worse," the man on her right said.

She still couldn't wrap her mind around any of this. But there was no time to debate it.

The blonde man grinned at her—but it only held malice. "You've run away. We aren't giving you what you need? You wasting and going over to some other place? That just won't do Ruth."

Karen shook her head. "I own this place. And I require myself to be freed at once. I run weddings, not reenactments."

Her eyes blurred with tears as she tried to reason with this man. She looked around at the faces staring back at her. The sea of Black faces. Some soft with youth and others filled with lines.

The man's face blotched red as he grabbed her wrists, wrapped them around a thick wooden log, and tied them with rope. . A whipping post. Horror churned in her belly. A nightmare. This had to be a nightmare.

She saw the man grab a whip with pieces of glass glittering in the sun.

"See Ruth here as an example!"

He brought the whip down on her exposed back and Karen saw spots in her vision while screaming. The whip and glass tore into her back and down her tights. He brought it down with the skill of someone with great practice. She struggled against her restraints and cursed who ever had put her here. She wasn't a slave—no—she merely owned the land where they used to be kept.

The pain drove her delirious—as people begged for someone to save her soul.

Karen wasn't sure how many times that whip was brought down her back. She felt the blood—sticky and hot—run down her back.

"Bring the salt," the man said.

Karen could barely process his words. Her whole body slumped and she panted.

She opened her eyes and surveyed those staring. Her eyes fixated on a familiar face.

Mack. His face was unlined and round—in the middle of transitioning from youth to adult. While he looked young, those eyes were not. The trickster remained.

"You," Karen whispered. "Did...this...to...me."

Mack ambled over and bent down so he was at her head. "You did it to yourself. Now Ruth is living in your world—able to have a life."

Karen muttered, "I am not her. This is wrong."

Mack smiled. "But that isn't how anyone else sees you."

Karen kneeled in the dirt, bracing herself and trying not to move.

She heard footsteps. "You—get her down. Lay her flat."

Karen didn't try to fight as she was laid out along the ground. She didn't have the strength to move. She kept muttering, "I'm not Black. I'm not a slave."

The man rubbed the salt into her bleeding back, sending Karen into a new frenzy of screaming and bucking. Karen wished for death—for something and anything to halt this suffering.

Mack watched, shaking his head. He looked at the men who'd held her—at the one with the jagged scar. Cumberland, who used to be Colin, remembered finding himself in the same place at a different time.

Ruth glanced around at the remnants of the wedding. She looked down at her new body and a grin overtook her face.

Mack appeared at her shoulder, startling her. "You get to decide what happens here. Keep it or sell it."

Ruth looked around at the land, how similar and foreign it felt to her. She closed her eyes and felt the wind caress her face. She lived here for a long enough time and reckoned that it was time to move on. Looking at the buildings daily seemed too painful. Places like this needed to exist, but Ruth didn't want to be the one tending to it.

"Put it up for sale," she said. "I don't think this is my home anymore."

AUTHOR NOTE

The main driving force of "Karma Karen" was anger and a deadline. The deadline to submit forced me to create my own inspiration instead of waiting for something to find me. I decided to think of the different threads that connect today to the past. And then, while scrolling online, I ran across a photo of people taking wedding photos in former slave quarters. I'd found my inspiration. I used anger to break apart how we view history. A time of opulence, pretty dresses, and picturesque landscapes fades into a reality of terror. America's collective memory of the past is short and fractured, so that's where the short story was birthed from. Enjoy?

AUTHOR BIOGRAPHY

Kristian Beverly has loved books and horses since she was young. A native of Pennsylvania, Kristian loves to read a bit of everything and ride whatever is thrown her way. She is the creative director of an independent bookstore. Combining her two loves allows Kristian to share her love of equines and reading with the community and world at large. In her free time, you'll find Kristian reading a book or riding a horse.

4

Faeries in the World

Elizabeth Koerber

As I walk through these woodlands I wonder-
Could there be magic here?
A door to Faerie Land?
Or perhaps the faeries are already here
Hiding from the human gaze.
Perhaps one day they will reveal themselves to my eyes
If I keep
Dreaming
Hoping
Believing

The Flying Cat

Elizabeth Koerber

Annika the cat looked around Cupboard Maker Books, the bookstore where she lived. It was a nice place to live, but she was getting tired of it. It seemed as if things never changed. She sighed as the door opened, and another person entered the store. The customer browsed the shelves, chose some books, paid for them, and left again.

Annika sat right next to the door as the customer left wishing everyone wouldn't be so careful about not allowing the cats to get out. Annika was very curious about the world outside her shop. Of course she could see things through the windows, but she wanted to see more of the world than that. It got very boring being trapped in the same place day in and day out. Annika saw the same shelves over and over again, and the views out the windows didn't change much either. She walked the same floors and walkways every day. She even slept in the same spots.

Annika supposed she might get some variety if she interacted more with customers, but she had no desire to do that. What she wanted to do was get outside and explore the world.

Today she felt even more restless than usual. "Have you ever wanted to leave this store?" she asked Squeekie.

Squeekie looked surprised at the question. "No. The people here love us and take care of us. Why would I want to leave?"

"I don't mean permanently," Annika said. "I just want to get out and see the world."

"You can see the world through the windows," Squeekie pointed out.

"I want to see more of the world than that," Annika grumbled. "In fact, I want to see the world from above. I want to grow wings and fly!"

Squeekie seemed startled. "I don't think cats can grow wings."

"Of course they can't," Annika replied grumpily. "I need to make a wish to grow wings and have it granted."

Squeekie now looked bemused. "How do you get a wish granted?"

"I need to find a genie in a lamp," Annika replied authoritatively. "They grant wishes."

Squeekie glanced up at the light fixtures in the bookstore. "I don't think we have lamps here."

"Not that kind of lamp," Annika told him. "A magic lamp."

"What does a magic lamp look like?" Squeekie wanted to know.

"I don't know," Annika admitted. "We can find out by listening to the humans talking. We'll see if they say anything about genies, magic lamps, or wishes."

Squeekie and Annika listened to the humans who came into the store hoping to hear about magic, genies, lamps, or granting wishes.

The first people Annika listened to were a mother and her daughter. They were looking at the children's books.

"Do you see any books you'd like?" the mother asked.

The little girl's eyes were wide. "I want all of them!"

Her mother laughed. "We can't get all the books, honey. We'll just pick out a few."

The girl opened her mouth to reply, but then she spotted Annika watching them.

"Mommy, a kitty!" she exclaimed and started running towards Annika.

Annika turned around and ran away. She had no desire to be manhandled by an enthusiastic child. From that point on she tried to listen to people from a spot where she couldn't be seen.

Two men walked into the store talking about a golf game and a fishing trip. Annika liked fish, but the conversation told her nothing about getting her wish granted.

One day she heard a woman exclaim, "I wish!"

Annika ran in the direction of the conversation hoping to hear something useful. There were two women talking.

"I wish," Annika heard the woman repeat. "I wish my husband looked this good!" She was holding a romance novel and gazing at the cover.

"I wish my husband looked half that good!" the second woman replied.

"Look at this one!" the first woman said as she pulled another romance book off the shelf.

Annika walked away leaving the women to their conversation. The phrase 'I wish' had given her high hopes, but this conversation was as useless as all the others.

After listening to more people Annika was starting to get grumpier than usual because she wasn't learning anything to help get her wish granted.

Then one day things changed.

Annika was sitting on one of the walkways around the ceiling of the store, still listening for useful information. Then she overheard a conversation between two female customers.

"Look at this shiny penny I found on the ground!" the first woman said. She held up the round, copper coin.

"Wow, a lucky penny!" replied the second woman. "Have you used it to make a wish yet?"

"Not yet," the first woman answered.

That was all Annika needed to hear. In a flash she was down from her walkway and running toward the two women. While the first woman was still holding up the penny Annika leaped into the air and knocked it on the ground. She immediately slapped her paw on the penny and thought "I wish to grow wings so I can go outside and explore!"

As soon as Annika finished making her wish she was nudged aside by one of the humans who worked at the store. They picked up the penny and handed it back to the customer. "I'm sorry about that. I don't know what got into Annika."

Annika just shook herself and walked to the back of the store. She didn't care what anyone thought. She had made her wish, and she was sure it was going to be granted. Soon she would have her wings!

When Annika told Squeekie he looked closely at her.

"Nothing's happening," he said. "I don't see any wings growing."

"Of course not," Annika stated. "The wings won't appear right now. The humans would wonder where they came from. They'll grow after the store closes for the day."

That night after the bookstore closed and all the humans were gone Squeekie and Annika sat together and waited expectantly.

However an hour later nothing had happened. Annika still didn't have wings.

"Maybe the lucky penny was defective or not really lucky," Squeekie suggested.

Annika wasn't ready to give up yet. "It has to work!" she exclaimed. "Maybe it just needs more time. I'll have wings in the morning. I'm sure of it."

Squeekie simply shrugged, wished Annika good luck, and curled up in his favorite bed by the window to sleep. Annika also settled down, and it wasn't long before she was sleeping too.

The next morning Annika woke up and stretched. She stretched each leg and arched her back. And as she arched her back, she felt something emerge. She looked and joy surged through her.

"Wings! I've got wings!" she exclaimed. She raced through the bookstore calling for Squeekie.

"What's going on?" he wanted to know.

Annika proudly unfurled her wings for him to see. Then she flapped them a few times and was elated to feel herself rising off the floor.

"My wish was granted!" she proclaimed happily.

Squeekie was speechless for a minute as he stared at Annika's wings.

"That's incredible!" he finally said.

"And look," Annika told him as she landed and folded in the wings, "they blend perfectly with my fur."

When she folded her wings in it was impossible to tell she had them. The humans would never find out her secret as long as she kept them folded in.

Annika turned and headed to the front door of the bookstore with her wings spread as she walked. The store was closed for a holiday so she knew no humans would show up.

"Now for the second part of my wish. I want to go outside."

Squeekie followed Annika, but when they go to the door she stopped short with a gasp.

"It's closed," Squeekie said.

Annika glared at him. "I can see it's closed. But it shouldn't be. I wished to go outside! I thought my wish would be granted by the door magically being open."

Still glaring Annika angrily swiped a paw at the door. To her shock the paw went right through the door as if it wasn't even there.

Squeekie put his paw up to the door, but it was solid for him. "It only seems to work for you," he told Annika.

"It only needs to work for me," Annika responded. Then she walked through the door and left the bookstore.

Once outside she flapped her wings and flew up to the roof of the building. Annika marveled at her view. She could see so much: roads and cars and shops and people. There were even railroad tracks!

Wanting an even better view Annika took off from the roof and went higher into the air. She found that she instinctively knew how to move with the air currents and how to hold her body so it would be easiest to fly. Annika swooped, dipped, rolled, and practiced all manner of flying. And all the while she looked at everything in sight. She was thrilled.

A few hours later she finally landed and reentered the bookstore. Annika found Squeekie waiting for her.

"I'm so glad you're back!" he exclaimed. "I was worried about you."

"There was nothing to worry about," Annika replied. "It was great! Squeekie, I love flying! I'm going to do it a lot from now on. When the bookstore is closed, of course. And I saw so much. I saw people. I know the humans say I don't like people, but I really do. I love watching people. What I don't like is when they also watch me. Or follow me around the store, try to pet me, or even worse attempt to pick me up." Annika shuddered. "When I'm up in the air I can watch people without them noticing me. It's wonderful!"

"Are you going to be nicer to people in the store now that you have a place to be where you can watch people without being bothered?" Squeekie wanted to know.

Annika gave him a bewildered look. "Why would I do that? I have to keep the people here in line. If I was nicer I would have even more people trying to touch me!" Annika shook her head. "Now I'm tired from flying. I'm going to take a nap. See you later Squeekie." And Annika sauntered off to find a good place to sleep.

Annika was true to her word about flying more. From that day on she flew as much as she could. Before the store opened, after it closed, and on holidays Annika was often in the air exploring the world around the shop. She always made sure to return to the store early enough that none of the employees missed her, and she was extra careful to never spread her wings when she was inside the store.

Annika also learned about weather. She discovered that flying in rain, sleet, or snow was not fun at all, and she quickly learned to stay inside on days with bad weather. Flying on sunny or cloudy days was fine though. In the warm weather she got a nice breeze while she soared through the air. When it was cold outside she didn't notice the cold while she enjoyed her flights. If she ever got tired there were plenty of buildings and trees where she could land and rest.

Annika wasn't the only animal in the air either. She talked to many birds. They seemed surprised to see a flying cat, but once their surprise passed they advised Annika on the different landscapes in the area. Armed with information from other animals Annika decided to explore the world around her in earnest. Before she had been flying without a particular destination in mind. Now she was really going to explore the world.

The train tracks across the street from the store intrigued her, and Annika decided to follow them and see where they led. She took two days first following them in one direction then the other. Annika flew as long as she could, but the tracks seemed to go on forever.

Finally, she realized she wasn't going to be able to find the end of the tracks and abandoned that idea.

The next time Annika flew she investigated a river. She didn't like water but seeing it from above wasn't bad. As she flew, she noticed a bird with long legs wading in the river. She landed on the riverbank near the bird to get a better look. She walked up to the bird being careful to stay on the bank and not to get her paws wet.

"Hello," Annika greeted it. "Who are you?"

The bird glanced at Annika. He didn't seem at all surprised to see a cat on the riverbank. "I'm a Great Blue Heron," the bird told her. He wasn't very interested in Annika and after answering he ignored her. Then suddenly he dipped his head in the water and came up with a fish.

Annika was very impressed. "Catching a fish like that is amazing!" she exclaimed.

The heron looked Annika up and down. "The water is pretty shallow here. Come on in, and I bet you can catch a fish too."

"Oh no," Annika replied shaking her head. "I do not like water or getting wet. I'll just stay here."

The heron accepted that and after a minute dipped his head in the water again. He came up with another fish and tossed it on the ground in front of Annika.

"Enjoy," he told her as he spread his wings and took off.

Annika was very grateful and devoured the fish. It was delicious.

On other days Annika went looking for people to watch. She discovered the best places to see people were store parking lots. People went in and out of the stores quite often, and Annika could watch all of them. If there was a big enough tree nearby Annika hid in the branches and watched. If no tree was available Annika simply watched from the top of the building. She discovered people hardly ever looked up.

Residential areas were good places to see people too. There were often more trees for Annika to hide in and watch everyone. Some people were outside, and others were inside. Annika found she could see through the windows in some places and observe people in their houses. She was amazed at all the people. She was seeing so many more than she would have seen if she had stayed inside the bookstore.

During her observations Annika discovered that children were more interesting to watch than adults. They were more energetic, and they were often doing more interesting things. In the store Annika avoided kids because they tended to try to pet and hold her. But when she was just watching them from a ways away they were fun to look at.

Annika also made sure to never let people see her. She never took off if she saw people watching or looking in her direction.

As careful as she was, some people did spot her. Some people thought they were imagining things, but others believed. Before long there were urban legends and rumors about a flying cat spreading. No one seemed to get a good look, and no one could agree on what the flying cat actually looked like. Some people swore it was a calico. Others swore it was a black cat. Still others insisted they saw an orange tabby flying. Customers in Cupboard Maker Books sometimes discussed the stories about a flying cat being seen. None of the staff had ever seen the flying cat, but they found the urban legend intriguing.

Annika listened to all the stories with amusement. Occasionally she pictured the looks on people's faces if she spread her wings in front of them. She never did that though. She liked her anonymity too much.

AUTHOR BIOGRAPHY

Elizabeth has always enjoyed writing, and she has written many stories. However, this is only her second published work. She also enjoys reading and reads about 100 books per year. Her favorite genre to write and read is fantasy. In addition to reading and writing she spends her time singing with the Harrisburg Choral Society and volunteering at her local library. She has a bachelor's degree in French from Randolph-Macon Woman's College and a Master of Science degree in Library and Information Science from the University of Tennessee. Elizabeth grew up in Central Pennsylvania, and then lived in Virginia, Tennessee, and Georgia before returning to Central Pennsylvania again. She lives with her mother, who she takes care of. She is also a huge cat lover and constantly spoils Lyre, her 12 year old tabby.

6

Fivel's Wedding Night

Joel Burcat

A hot, *schvitzy*, dark suit, white shirt, necktie, black hat wedding dance. The mob of men—pushing, shoving, dancing in concentric circles. The music—loud and pulsating. The clarinet— urges them forward. The women—are elsewhere. Not here. That is not permitted. It could lead to...dancing.

Dance with wild abandon my *havers*, my friends. The music pulls them onward. Twirling, legs extended. Some kind of crazy footwork. A St. Vitus dance fueled by vodka, whiskey, and joy.

Suddenly, it's syncopated. Eight men, dancing in a circle, the same mad, spontaneous step—leg in, kick out, shrug, jump. Again. They press each other forward, more wild, more intense. Holding each other up, hand-to-hand, hand-to-shoulder. Following the beat. It's not possible to go faster, to be more insane. Laughing. Singing. Tribal. Like hunters, rejoicing after a kill. Victorious. Like soldiers, returning from a mission. Alive.

Yankel desperately searches for Fivel, the *hasen*. The bridegroom. Frantic. Yankel has been his study partner in *yeshiva* since they were thirteen. Twelve hours a day. He glimpses Fivel in the center of it all, the hub of the circles. He lurches through the horde to reach him.

Perspiration flows freely. Buckets of it. A few black jackets carelessly tossed aside. The white shirts, slick. And those hats! Black fedoras. Genuine fur felt. Pure Borsalino. Pure 1940s. Wide brims. No porkpie—heaven forbid. Sweat trickles out from under, down necks, down beards, coats the *tzit-tzit* fringes that have escaped from under the shirts. Drenched, they slap to the beat.

The elders dance in the outermost, slowest, circle, eyes shut, trance-like. Feeling the music. Remembering when they danced in the innermost ring. Drawn forward by the man whose liver-spotted hand he holds in front of him. Pulling along the man behind him. There he is—the father of the bride. His daughter! Nineteen. He's lost in another world. Another time. Another place. Tearfully awaiting this day. His *Shaynaleh*. His pretty little one. Happy. Nervous. Scared.

The music is endless. Thirty, forty, fifty minutes. Play. Repeat. Again. A high-energy Yiddish number. Biblical words played on a clarinet. A trumpet. The electric guitar fighting for the lead. *Shall there be heard...the voice of joy...voice of gladness...voice of the bridegroom... voice of the bride*. The men all sing along. Words etched in the medulla. Circle in a circle in a circle. Impossible to break through. Each circle moves at its own speed with its own persona. The song. On all their lips. The women peek through the tall curtain at the madness. And point.

Fivel. Twenty-one, twenty-two, not much older. Wearing the new black suit his father bought him at Mendy's on Thirteenth Avenue. Finally, holding hands and dancing with his best friend, Yankel, in a wild circle. It is his wedding night!

"Your bride is beautiful, Fivella," Yankel shouts above the din.

What pleasure awaits? They can only imagine. No, really, they can only imagine.

Yankel yearns to say something he's wanted to say for years, but cannot bring himself to do it. They kick ferociously. Wildly. Missing each other by millimeters. Laughing. Holding each other up with sweaty hands. Spinning faster than the others. It's just the two of them and nothing else.

A Chagall landscape: the couple floats above the village. Fivel and Yankel sing along loudly, although no one can hear them over the maelstrom. Whirling in a wild circle, laughing, tears streaming down glistening faces.

Others break into the groom's tight circle, grab hands and expand the circle first to four, then ten, then twenty men. Kicking wildly, dancing madly, Yankel and Fivel drift away.

It is his wedding night!

AUTHOR NOTE

I've always enjoyed the stories of Isaac Bashevis Singer. He combined folklore with deep insights into the human condition. I also love the art of Marc Chagall. He, too, combined folklore scenes with wild imagery, some of it realistic and some imagined, in beautiful Modernist paintings. Like Singer, there is another story beneath the surface of Chagall's work. This piece of flash fiction portrays a quintessential moment in the life of an Orthodox Jewish man—his wedding. In all Jewish Ultra-Orthodox weddings and most Orthodox weddings these days, the men and women are separated by a curtain or wall and do not dance together. Instead, both dance folk-dance style in concentric circles. If you can Google a recording of klezmer music, preferably the song *Od Yishama*, that would be the perfect accompaniment to reading this story. Loosely based on a real event, my story combines elements of both Singer and Chagall. Like both of their works, something else is going on here. It is with a sense of humility that I wrote my story with their stories and artwork in mind.

AUTHOR BIOGRAPHY

Joel Burcat is a novelist and environmental lawyer. His debut novel, DRINK TO EVERY BEAST, about midnight dumping, was the first in his series of Mike Jacobs environmental legal thrillers. His second published novel and next in the series, is AMID RAGE, about strip mining, will be released on February 2, 2021.

He has received the following awards: Second Place, PennWriters (Novel Beginnings, 2020); Quarterfinalist, ScreenCraft 2019 Cinematic Book Competition; Honorable Mentions at N.Y. Book Festival 2019 (for Best General Fiction) and 2019 Readers' Favorite (for Fiction-Legal Thriller). In addition, he has a number of short stories that have been published in literary magazines and anthologies.

Burcat was selected as the 2019 Lawyer of the Year in Environmental Litigation (for Central PA) by Best Lawyers in America. He has also received "Super Lawyers" and "Best Lawyers" designations for environmental and energy law and was selected by the Pa. Bar Association as a recipient of its annual award in environmental law

Burcat is a Philadelphia native and now lives in Harrisburg, Pa. with his wife, Gail. They have two grown daughters, a son-in-law and granddaughter.

7

The Sad and Bloody Stones of Kerrigan's Keep

Robert E. Furey

When I was much younger, I'd not been a believer. My universe articulated quite nicely, organized and comprehensible. But yes, stories abounded with shadows slouching through the dark places. History brims with such tales. I'd seen these stories as guideposts, beckoning fingers enjoining me to youthful adventures, no more than secret maps to locations far off-trail. I've gone to many such places, when I was younger. I'm different now.

When my great uncle was just a boy from Oranmore, a village outside Galway, he had been detained by leprechauns. Or so the family story goes. He had climbed into the cellar of an old stone cottage, a place he had been told not to go. When he attempted to exit at his mother's call to dinner the little people emerged from the walls and stopped him. When finally they'd allowed him to leave, midnight had come and gone. He received a terrible whipping. Not solely for climbing into the abandoned cellar, but for lying and blaming the leprechauns.

All his life he never wavered in his claim, until even when on his deathbed, well into his 80s, he grabbed his son's collar to pull him close. "It's all true," he said with his very last breath.

This is a family story. My great uncle's generation believed it. My parents' generation nodded and winked; some gave it a tolerant chuckle. As for my generation, they forgot. But not me - I did not forget.

I'd found an old book years before. It would be dishonest for a story's sake to refer to this book as if it had the appearance of a grimoire or some arcane hornbook. Poor taste to imply that it was bound in some suspiciously soft and fine leather. It wasn't. The book, still sitting on my shelf, is clothbound with a time-dulled acorn-squash and tan cover. Tendrils of fraying threads snake from the spine. A squat crudely drawn map of Ireland, much wider than tall, extends oddly from the inside cover across the first page.

As distorted as the map clearly was, it still held clues to what I looked to find, interesting and little-seen places. That is to say, guideposts toward the locations with stories attached. History that insisted on being heard. History that refused to die. Not that I ever expected to find anything as much as experience a place where a story got its start. And if there were anywhere in the world where these stories would enrich my experience, it would be the Old Sod where bits of my DNA swirled through the island's blood.

"We're gonna find such cool shit there, I might just stay," I said. Drawing my thumbnail across my upper lip, I swiped away the foam from my last quaff of Guinness. I already felt the spirit.

Brad nodded, smiling, then took his own deep gulp of stout. "That part's up to you. I just want to go to Ireland and see some of that cool shit you keep talking about." He swept his pint glass toward the open book sitting on the varnished tabletop. "So, let's plan."

The map had long since faded into the page, contrasting weakly with the time-yellowed paper. The pub's hanging Tiffany lamps, designed with harps, shamrocks, and brass-buckled high hats -- Ireland's own cultural invasion -- spread colored shadows through the violet clouds of tobacco smoke. Spinning the book toward me, I squinted at the hand-penned town names. This was not the first time we'd spoken about the goal, and a name that seemed to rise again.

I'd been open about my great uncle's story and gave the supernatural aspects of the trip a nod. I downplayed it, so as not to seem off, but the fact is I talked about hauntings and fey all through our plans. Brad never really took it seriously. And that was fine. But I wanted to see...something. And ghost stories were easy to find. But I wasn't interested in the fleeting shadow of a widow's spirit watching from a high window, or the shadowy wisps of some eternal wedding party gliding along garden paths. I found myself drawn to something more.

"Somewhere in there," I said, jabbing at the map between the names Kinvarra and Ballyvaughn, "Kerrigan's Keep. I still vote for Kerrigan's Keep."

At a time in Ireland when all that was needed to be a king was a castle and someone to fight, Kerrigan built his battlements on the Atlantic coast and quickly got to the business of bloodshed. During a treaty negotiation at his castle, Kerrigan murdered a visiting king and all his gallowglass retainers. Then he had his men inter the bodies under the floor stones in the keep and conceal the treachery of his actions.

A tale unforgotten is still a tale for today. It is said that across the centuries their murders at the hands of Kerrigan's men has served to bind those fallen to the earth. Exorcists and adventurers sought out the Keep and the souls trapped within. For each that disturbed the uneasy resting place, the slain gallowglasses rose up in red-hot hatred. They assaulted careless adventurers, and those few that managed to escape death fell to madness. But if eyeless sockets cannot clearly discern friend from foe, the dead should be forgiven for that. Although now I see mercy for the living may be too much to ask even of those who have conquered death.

Storytellers recounting the tale of Kerrigan's Keep must have changed the details down through the centuries. It is something the Irish do. But even so, the Keep is there, and something did happen inside. The book said things still happen today. I dismissed the hyperbole.

"Kerrigan's Keep it is!" he said. We saluted Kerrigan with raised pint glasses.

We rendezvoused in Paris and left by car for Ireland. Somewhere along the way La Manche became the English Channel, then beyond to the Straits of Saint George and the Irish Sea. Finally, the car rolled down the iron ramps in Ireland, leaving the sleek-hulled catamaran behind for Dublin's cobbled streets.

A large banner fluttered over the departure ramp, "Fáilte!" it welcomed in runic lettering. Ireland has experienced a reawakening of interest in its culture, from the inside as well as out. In spite of finding ourselves one car in a long line of tourists, the douane officer told me, "Welcome home," as he returned my passport.

We drove to town and walked along the waterfront while waiting for the banks to open their exchange bureau. Delivery trucks, or lorries now I suppose, rumbled along cobbled streets. Drivers, whose hats slung at precise angles sat close to their scalps, lugged huge trays of steaming bread or dented aluminum kegs. And everywhere English transformed to music by the brogue.

"Oh, man, look at that," Brad said. A slow-moving line snaked along the sidewalk. "We should've come by the bank right away. Let's go."

The sudden and unexpected crush of tourists at the exchange bureau promised to keep us in line for over an hour. But we had only just arrived in Ireland and so I for one felt no need to rush.

"We'll be out of town soon enough," I said. "Outside the city it'll be better. Stick with the plan. Stick with the plan."

For me just being in Ireland held magic. I didn't need more.

Once we folded our handfuls of new Irish Punts into our wallets we went directly to a tiny corner restaurant. The tables were chock-a-block and the air surprisingly thick with American, British, and French accents. I'd come for Gaelic and found all but that.

After a heavy Irish Breakfast, we took the winding road west toward Limerick. Outside of Rosslare we saw directions to the new John Fitzgerald Kennedy Arboretum. The world loves JFK, and the Irish would beatify him if they could. Later, entering Limerick, we drove along the reconstructed battlements of King John's Castle. The ancient battlements, fortified with muzzled cannon, brooded over the city, glaring across the River Shannon. This had been one of the last strongholds of British rule in the Republic, and yet the Irish have rebuilt it as well. For the tourists.

Ireland's roads were not designed to accommodate the number of cars descending from the Continent. Each town and attraction funneled traffic to the main arteries where movement tended to slow to a halt.

"This isn't what I expected," I said, tapping my claddagh ring against the steering wheel.

"I don't know, man. Maybe we want to stop at a few of the sights along the way? It's better than slogging from one traffic jam to the next." Brad wrestled with a map, refolding to a new section up the coast.

"I think we ought to stick with the plan for now," I said. "We might not find Kerrigan's right off. And that's the goal."

"We're here and blowing past a lot of things looking for some ruins we don't even know still exist or not."

I didn't respond immediately. He was right, I knew that. Peering ahead for some break in the jam, I saw little respite through the exhaust and noise. "We can see whatever we want on the way back."

He groaned, frustrated with the traffic or my response, I couldn't tell. Double-decked tour busses stopped in the road or no, I focused on keeping the car rolling ahead as best I could.

In early afternoon we pulled up to the Cliffs of Mohar. Past the crowded souvenir shop, we hung our heads over the granite precipice above the sea. Fog-laden winds blew in from the Atlantic where the cliffs redirected them into a vertical river of heavy cloud, as if a rent had opened in reality. Wheeling seagulls faded in and out of the mist like fey voyagers through curtains between worlds. In those moments Kerrigan's Keep felt very close. I sent postcards of the cliffs from the kiosk on the way out, of course. It's what you do.

For the rest of the afternoon we hugged the coast road until arriving at the freshly painted town of Ballyvaughn. Here we took our second stop, for food, directions, and a campsite. I'd thought the final leg to the Keep might be on the following day. Then we got a break.

We pulled into a restaurant just before a group of masked Japanese tourists took the remaining tables. When I mentioned Kerrigan's, the waiter that served us the steamed fish and potatoes knew exactly where we needed to go.

"Sure I know where is the Keep. 'Tis a dark place people should've left alone," he said as he placed a pint of black porter in front of each of us.

Brad snorted. "We better find something after missing all we missed."

"We've come a long way." I told him. "Too far to turn back now." I waited for more of the story from the waiter, but he just stood there. After taking a long swallow of stout, I continued: "We want to see for ourselves if the story about..."

"I know well the story," he interrupted, nodding his head. For a moment he fixed his gaze on me. "I see the very map of Ireland in your face, boyo. Don't go there."

I looked over at Brad, who wolfed down his fish, and back to the waiter. Something twisted through the pit of my stomach, and the porter I emptied into myself never seemed to hit bottom.

"It's close I'd guess?" I said. I'd hoped to change the tone and coax out a little more information.

"Go home," he said. "Go home and keep your dreams intact. What's happened there is a terrible sin."

At that point, and with some relief, I knew we were talking about the same place. "All that was a long time ago. Whatever sin happened, at some point it has to die."

"You'd think." The waiter wiped his hands before looking at me again. "You don't want to go there."

I watched him move away through the small table-crowded restaurant, blending back into the brouhaha. "What the fuck was that?"

"What the fuck was what?" Brad asked. He reached for his pint.

I told him what the waiter said, that the Keep was dangerous and we shouldn't go there.

"Whatever. I don't even care anymore if there really are ghosts. As long as we finally stop long enough to see something on this trip."

The more I thought about it, the less I wanted to let a stranger frighten me with vague worries about sin. He'd probably gone back to the kitchen and laughed with his buddies.

Later, the dreary gray sky seemed to reach down and press against our shoulders as we pitched the tent. We set up camp in a tiny patch of lawn squeezed between two in-town houses, crammed amid dozens of other gaudy, nylon dome and A-frame tents. Heavy mist had soaked us both to the skin by the time we crawled inside and zipped away the night.

In the morning, we wandered through the small village to a tea-room with a huge gravel parking lot. A tour bus had just pulled in and disgorged whorls of huddled Japanese tourists from the night before. They all wanted scones and Irish breakfast tea, leaving the espresso machine free for us. We gulped hot coffee and hurried back to the car.

Between the map and the back-handed encouragement from the waiter, I felt confident we would find the old castle. We drove away from Ballyvaughn and into the surrounding hills. The road got smaller the farther into the Burren we pressed, and lonelier.

Ireland rolled to the sea in great fractured slabs of stone and tumbles of shattered boulders. Anchored in scattered pockets of topsoil, brave trees bent to the perpetual wind from the ocean in twisted, hunching shapes. Clouds of heavy mist scuttled over the stone across this remnant of Ireland's spectacular desolation.

Away from the crowds, away from the busses and traffic, far from the pandering, the Burren seemed immune to the invasion from the outside world. And there rose the lichen-covered tower of Kerrigan's Keep. As we rolled through the foothills, it dipped beneath the mist-bathed horizon, to jut into view again as we topped the next rise. As if the keep heaved in and out of time.

And then we drove up to the sign.

"Welcome to Kerrigan's Keep," it proclaimed in bold green lettering. "Come see the haunted Castle!"

For me this seemed the final, crushing disappointment. The garish sign a blasphemy against the rocky land and the stony walls of the keep.

"Shit, Brad," I said, "so much for that."

"Come on, man. It's a castle." He tilted in close to the windshield.

At that moment I realized that I had been following a quest while Brad had been on vacation. And in a large way, we had both failed. "Maybe, but so much for being lost and off the beaten trail."

53

As we pulled close to the goal I'd held so long, my heart thumped hard against my ribs. At least Kerrigan's Keep did exist, very much as I had pictured it. A crumbling tower alone in the broad expanse of shattered landscape. Tumbles of building stones scattered away from the long-fallen outer castle walls.

Only there was more. We found the ruins flanked by a new asphalt parking lot, souvenir shop, and soft ice-cream stand. We parked in the still empty lot and wandered toward a corrugated aluminum ticket booth. A Sky News truck, generator running, was parked near a Grand Opening sign.

There was a ten-punt entry fee, expensive but we paid. After the freckle-faced girl stuffed our bills into a shiny new strongbox, she smiled. She pointed toward a hole in the stone wall. Steps descended into shadows within the Keep.

"Right through there, with ye," she said. "Don't be too afraid." She kept smiling for us.

Brad leaned forward. "Just how scary is it inside?" he asked, clearly flirting with the Irish girl.

"Oh, it's not for the likes of me down there," she said. She produced a dramatic shudder following up with a wink.

Brad ate it up.

The steps disappeared downward into darkness. Maybe the same darkness I'd been searching for since before we'd ever left home.

My hand slid down a shiny handrail affixed to the old stone walls. Fresh mortar showed white in the gaps between the rocks of the tunnel wall. A deep-red glow suffused the approaching chamber, lit as if not to disturb sleeping bats. Our rubber-soled hiking boots squeaked on the time-polished granite steps.

Despite my preparation for this descent, when the rumbling began my footsteps faltered. And when the moaning started, I stopped outright. Shaking built up strong in my arms and legs until I had to grip the rail to stay on my feet. I saw Brad had stopped too. As we exchanged glances my breath hissed through my clenched teeth. I could have turned around then. But I didn't.

"What the hell..." Brad gripped the railing with both hands. "That ain't fake." He turned and bounded up the flight of steps, leaving a "Come on!" in his wake.

Me, I couldn't turn back. When I found myself alone on the descent, I felt the history of Ireland waited below. In hindsight I can't be sure what frightened me most, but it drew me on. Something wanted to see me. And my feet seemed to take those final steps of their own accord.

They were still boiling from the earth when I reached the bottom of the stairway. Stones flew through the air and crashed against a thick barrier of plexiglass erected between our world and theirs.

Waves of hatred and despair washed over me from those expressionless bone faces. Rusted weapons pulverized and skeletons fell to dust battering against the barrier wall. Those warriors reintegrated to hurl themselves at it again. They were prevented from enacting terrible vengeance only by the thick plexiglass barrier. Recoiling, I watched the cycle of disintegration and resurrection roil impotently against the plastic. I watched until I wept.

My great uncle had been true all along. The fey existed. Most had left a changing world, but a few we'd chased down.

And no, before you ask, they did not frighten me, those ember-eyed revenants. I stood watching them, my fingertips pressed against the plexiglass wall. I was acutely aware of the banners snapping outside the refurbished keep, the flickering shadows of bloody neon glow within. The scents of time and mortar filled my head. I would have released the warriors if I could. Freeing them would have been right. A world guilty of betraying such devotion and honor, more powerful than the passage of time, did not deserve them.

I turned away from the onslaught against the barrier. I mounted the stairway as a tour bus pulled into the Keep's new asphalt parking area. The Japanese tourists from the village had arrived. With their mouths covered by cotton air filters and with cameras swinging from neck tethers, they flowed past me as if I wasn't there. In the darkness below, the viewing chamber soon filled with their chattering and the whirring of electronic cameras. That cacophony almost - almost - drowned the frenzy from beyond the wall.

As I exited the keep the pounding on the plexiglass grew louder. I pondered my own betrayal in leaving them there, ensnared. Their anguished devotion that transcended even time, exploited for greed and trapped in a plastic cage. I still hear them pounding. And I fear I always will.

AUTHOR NOTE

I must say that every word of the above story is true, except where it deviates, and even then remains true through metaphor. In the summer 1996 I'd been living in France for a year or so when my friends Brad and Angela came to visit and we made the road trip from Nancy, France to Ireland. Over the years we had talked many times about finding Kerrigan's Keep. The keep was not the focus of the voyage but certainly sat high on our Irish walkabout Bucket List. There were four of us on that trip, along with Brad and Angela, there was me of course, and an ex-girlfriend. In the story you will find only two people – the only part of the story that is false. As for the rest, all of it's true, even if some is between-the-lines truth.

Robert E. Furey

AUTHOR BIOGRAPHY

Rob is a professor teaching behavioral ecology, forensics, and writing at Harrisburg University, and has been the forensic entomologist at the Dauphin County Coroner's Office for the past 15 years. He writes science, nonfiction, and genre fiction to keep his mind on an even keel. Rob and his wife Courtney live in a 200 year old farmhouse outside Harrisburg, PA with their easygoing dog, two imperial cats, and a very ornery macaw.

8

The Girl and the Stone Garden

Shawn Marie Mann

Tucked into a little clearing on the seaside sat a small cottage with three rooms. In that cottage lived a man, a woman and their daughter named Althea.

The man spent his days fishing for food for his village and his family. The woman spent her days tending the garden which provided plants for food and for healing. She also spent time teaching Althea about how to serve the Earth and her fellow man.

On Althea's seventh birthday in early spring her mother took her to a very special beach she had never seen before. The beach was filled with amazing stones that glittered in the sun. Each stone was egg shaped and they were every size from the tiniest grain of sand to a stone as large as her bed at home.

The tide rose and fell over those stones leaving behind pools of water.

"Look here Althea," said her mother. "Do you see all of the tiny fish here?"

Althea peeked into a pool and saw dozens of tiny fish. If she put her finger into the pool very slowly the fish nibbled on it with their tiny mouths and it tickled!

She looked around and saw pool after pool of water. In each one something was living – fish, crabs, snails – all kinds of tiny creatures.

"Why are they here Momma? Why all the little pools of babies?"

Her mother swept her arm the full length of the beach, "Because this is the Sea's nursery. This beach contains all of the baby creatures that will grow up to live in the Sea when they get bigger. It is a very special place, there is no other like it anywhere on this coast. And now that you are a big girl you can visit here any time you wish to make friends with the tiny creatures."

Althea thought the tiny fish were cute, but it was the stones that she couldn't get enough of. Pink ones, green ones and some of them were even blue and became transparent when the water hit them!

"Momma, may I take a stone home with me? They are so very beautiful."

Her mother thought for a moment, "Since it is your birthday you may choose one stone to go home with you as your very own. But that is all, you can never take another away from this beach. These stones must stay here. They belong to the Sea."

Althea nodded, "Yes, just one. I promise."

It took some time but finally she chose a white stone with pink crystals the size of her hand. It felt warm from the sun and smelled of the Sea. When she returned home, she placed the stone on a shelf next to her bed where she could see it while she was falling asleep. It almost seemed as if she could hear the Sea when she looked at it.

The next day Althea woke and looked at her stone. At breakfast she asked for permission to return to the beach. Her mother agreed but warned her once again, "Remember Althea, you have your stone now. You must take no more. You may look at them all you want, but they must stay on the beach."

"Yes, Momma," Althea replied and ran out of the house.

The forest path smelled green and damp, but she could hear the roar of the Sea through the trees. She ran faster and gasped again when she saw the glittering beach full of stones of every size and color and little ponds full of all the tiny creatures you could imagine.

She spent that day making friends with the tiny swimming things, talking to them and letting them know how exciting it would be when they got bigger and reached the giant Sea. The little creatures seemed to be listening to her and they always tickled her finger when she put it in the water.

With the sun full overhead, Althea knew it was time to return home for lunch. She took one last look at the beach and saw a particularly beautiful stone near her foot. It was one of the blue ones that looked like a piece of the sky had fallen to earth.

She picked it up and put it in her pocket. "One more tiny stone shouldn't hurt right? There are so many more out there on the beach."

Small voices whispered and said she should put it back, but she didn't listen.

She ran home through the forest and found her mother putting food on the table for lunch. "Welcome home Althea, how was the beach?"

"Beautiful Momma. The stones were sparkling and the little creatures were so friendly!" She washed her hands and felt the weight of the stone in her pocket. She wanted to confess to her mother she had taken it, but the words wouldn't come.

Her mother looked at her closely, "You didn't take another stone today did you Althea? They need to stay on the beach."

Althea shook her head and told the first lie of her life, "No Momma."

Her mother smiled, "Good. You can tell your father about your trip when he gets home tonight."

After lunch, her mother was in the house mending clothes but Althea went out into their garden. She knew she had to hide the stone someplace so her mother wouldn't find it and there was nowhere in the house to hide it.

She walked through every path on their land and finally she found a dark shady spot under a large fallen tree that would hide her stone. She removed the stone from her pocket and placed it gently under the tree. It didn't glitter in the dark like it did on the sunny beach, but it was still a beautiful shade of blue.

Happy with her hiding spot, Althea ran back to the house to help with the mending still not saying a word about the stone.

The next day she again visited the beach and played with the tiny Sea creatures and again found a stone too beautiful to leave behind. As she was leaving, she heard the voices again telling her to put it back, but she didn't listen to them. She again lied to her mother and she placed the pink stone next to the blue one near the tree in the garden.

Day after day, Althea visited the beach. She saw fewer and fewer pools of little creatures, but she was still able to find a beautiful stone every day to add to her garden. As time went on, the voices telling her to return the stone got softer until she couldn't hear them at all.

It had gotten easier to lie to her mother too. The entire area surrounding the tree was now covered in stones. She loved looking at the patterns she had made with the stones. It was her private garden and its beauty was for her alone.

As the year moved into late summer, Althea gathered the beautiful flowers in the garden. One day she rushed into the house with a bouquet of them to put on the table for supper.

Her mother served a vegetable stew and all three sat down to eat.

"I just don't understand it, I've had fewer and fewer fish in my nets these last few weeks." Her father looked sad. "We will have a hard time surviving the winter without fish if I can't catch more. It will be vegetable stew every day."

Her mother looked concerned, "Is it just your nets that have gone empty?"

He shook his head, "No. The whole village has lost most of their fish, the crabs too. Everything seems to be going away. I wish I knew why."

They finished their dinner and at bedtime Althea's mother tucked her in. She had a curious look on her face, but Althea didn't know why. Her mother asked, "Althea, have you seen many tiny creatures down at the beach on your trips? Are they still friendly with you?"

Althea thought about that for a moment and realized it had been a very long time since she saw ANY small creatures on the beach. "No Momma, the creatures have not been there."

A pained look crossed her mother's face. "Yet you still go every day to visit the beach?"

"Yes, Momma. The stones are so beautiful."

Her mother sighed, kissed her head and left the room.

The next morning Althea was getting ready to go to the beach when her mother stopped her at the door, "Let me put on my sweater and I will go with you. I need to breathe some Sea air."

They walked through the forest and out onto the beach. Her mother gasped when she saw that only three stones remained. Althea was surprised too. She hadn't realized she had taken so many.

She and her mother sat on the largest stone and her mother spoke very slowly to her. "Althea, the stones on this beach kept the pools of water safe for the tiny creatures to live in until they were big enough to go out into the Sea. Without those pools of water there are no new baby creatures."

Althea had a sick feeling inside. "And if there are no baby creatures, there are no big creatures for Father to catch are there?"

Her mother shook her head.

Althea realized what she had done. The voices she heard when she took the stones were her friends warning her not to take away their homes. She didn't listen to them and she didn't listen to her mother.

Not only had she lost her little friends by being greedy and taking the stones, but she had also endangered the lives of her village and her family by robbing the Sea of new life. All because she wanted the beautiful stones for her own garden.

It was time to tell the truth, "Momma. I've been taking the stones and I made a stone garden for myself with them in our garden. I'm sorry."

Her mother sighed, "Thank you for telling the truth. But you must now realize that the beautiful things the Earth provides are here for us all to share, not for only one person to keep for themselves. We must think of the other creatures who depend on the Earth's gifts as well."

Tears fell down Althea's cheeks.

Her mother sat thinking and then said, "We might be able to make things better if we put the stones back where they belong. Can you show me your stone garden?"

Althea grabbed her mother's hand and they ran back to their home and she showed her where her stone garden was.

Her mother turned to her, "These stones belong to the Sea. They don't belong here in this garden. Do you know what we must do Althea?"

Althea nodded, "Yes, we must return the stones to the beach and to the Sea."

For many days Althea and her parents returned the stones to the beach. Althea even returned the stone from the shelf in her room. She understood now that the stone was so much more than a pretty thing, it was part of the life of the creatures of the Sea and they needed it far more than she did.

Once the stones were returned, the Sea took over, cleaning the stones and rearranging them to her liking until the beach was back to its sparkling splendor. The tide pools were back as well, even more of them than before.

Each morning for many mornings Althea looked into the pools for little fishes or crabs or any signs that her friends were back. Each day she left for home disappointed.

Her mother hugged her, "Be patient. The Earth takes her time."

In the middle of autumn, Althea and her mother once again made a trip to the beach together. Althea still loved the glittering stones, but the empty pools made her sad. She sat with her mother on one of the largest stones and dangled her toes into a pool.

To her surprise, something – no, many somethings – nibbled at her toes. Her friends were back!

She ran from pool to pool, looking at the beautiful colors of her friends from the Sea. Tears of joy ran down her face to know the Earth had healed from her selfish mistake.

As she stood in the middle of the beautiful stone beach, she made the Sea and her friends a promise. "I'm sorry I didn't listen to everyone before about not taking the stones. But now I know how important they are to you. Never again will I take your beautiful stones for my own pleasure. The Earth, the Sea and your lives are far more important to me than that."

And to this day, the beach glitters with rounded stones and pools, filled with the babies of the Sea.

AUTHOR BIOGRAPHY

Shawn Marie Mann is a writer based in Central PA who lives with her kids, cats and giant goldfish. She writes about everything, anything and sometimes nothing at all. She enjoys amusement parks, Cupboard Maker Books, the Bold Coast of Maine and chocolate. You can reach her at shawnmariewrites@gmail.com.

9

Learning to Let Go

Kathyann Corl

To risk is to be able to act and to react to life
Yet in that risking unexpected change,

In the process of risking, the unexpected appears,
Confronting one's ability to react to life.
The ability to act without needing control
Requiring only the introspection, of being at peace with the Creator.

Engaging life can be an encounter
A process of living and dying
To be able to begin to live for the unexpected

Being able to touch life in the palm of the hand
Embracing this intimate relationship with Life's very existence
Evolves into a process of knowing and becoming.

Embracing life for the sake of Living
Engaging this moment with the Creator
Begins the process of loving and being loved.

Walk with me Lord
That I may know your loving forgiveness
That I may learn the process of Letting Go.

10

One Battle Lost, Another Begun

Kathyann Corl

This World as we know it has been destroyed by man in the Great Wars. The land has been devastated into an endless desert and the remaining survivors are living lives of extreme hopelessness.

Yet as so many are wandering across the deserts, the Creator has left a few to be the holders of faith.

Carol is a holder of the hope for this world. She is a fighter who fights for the beauty of the souls who she is called to care for. She never knows what direction she will go next. She just listens for the call to find the 'Chosen Ones.'

Carol is engaged in an ongoing battle of World War III to save the souls of the lost ones who meander through the earth's creation, planting seeds to help them grow.

With these seeds, she seeks to nourish the Chosen Ones so they will find their own path of wellness. Yet the seeds are not always recognized by the wanderers and all too often swept away before they ever have an opportunity to take root in the ground and grow.

Today Carol is troubled. It seems that the battle of transformation is wearing her down. It is hard to be a holder of hope for so many in the world.

In the last battle, the Chosen One was named TJ.

Carol spent much time walking the desert with him and sharing her seeds of wisdom. Yet TJ deliberately turned away from the gift she offered him. TJ exploded and lashed out. As they walked into the winds together TJ began walking into the innermost part of the wind's whirlwind – denying everything she said and running into the cyclone.

Carol had seen this happen too often. She knew at this point nothing she could say would make a difference. When people walked into this cyclone not even a glimmer of light could be reflected through the eternal darkness and endless pain.

Carol hastily pulled her veil over her face as she felt the velocity of the storm clouds beginning their swirling winds. Carol knew that she did not have the strength to offer any more seedlings. This 'Chosen One' would have to come to the Creator himself, in his own time.

So she walked away, filling her mind with prayers for TJ. She began to focus on the trickle of the sand between her toes. Slowly she began to collect sand, shells and crystals, each so miniscule, yet containing within them stories of their lives in the seas. Stories of how they now intermingled with the desert as they had once crossed the vast expanse of the ocean's floor.

These are the moments, Carol pondered, moments when she knew that all she had was this molecule of sand. It had been tossed by the ocean's waves, telling her that she had come home.

The winds continued to darken the sky, yet on she walked. She walked towards a glimmer of light in the distance. She walked and picked little gleanings of rush. She walked against the wind and the gleanings of wheat went into a large wicker basket. She walked into the light.

She began to feel the ocean breeze across her cheeks. Now the North Star shone overhead, glimmering its light into the twilight sky.

The evening skies darkened and she walked towards the light that shone across the sea of sand.

The light came from a weather worn lighthouse built many years ago. This lighthouse could still provide her shelter over the night despite its cracked walls.

Inside the lighthouse, Carol found a fire pit and dry twigs in corner. She used them to start the fire.

She found a large stone. With it she pounded and pounded the gleanings, then baked them into a small loaf of bread so she could nourish herself.

Carol took off her shawl and wondered where the Creator would send her next. Carol prayed for TJ as he seemed like such a lost soul. She prayed TJ would receive the Creator's wisdom from another wanderer. Perhaps there was hope that he would ruminate on the gifts she had given him and decide at some point to accept them.

The sky filled with millions of stars from the heavens. She slept the sleep of the just, knowing the Creator would give her the strength to face tomorrow's journey. She watched the flames of the fire dancing along the walls and reflected once more on her simple prayer of faith:

"All is well, All is well with my soul."

Kathyann Corl

AUTHOR NOTE

The inspiration for this story was when I reflected on the world that we are living in and how hard it can be to find hope in this world. I wanted to expand these thoughts into a futuristic world where we are living in a world and then discovering a world of devastation to find even a moment of hope where good could exist.

AUTHOR BIOGRAPHY

I have always had a love of writing since a young age starting with poetry and then moving into writing articles for local papers and editing. Through my employer I collected stories on mental health recovery which resulted in two books being created on the subject of Recovery. (Second book is due for publication in 2021)

11

Cursed

Jennifer Woodings

How had it come to this?

She wondered as she tried to calm her heart and catch her breath. Her back was pressed tight against the cave wall as she tried to find safety in the shadows of a small alcove. The cave had been her home for years now and she had finally begun to feel safe for the first time she could remember in an exceptionally long time. True, there had been some who had sought her out but she had been able to defend herself and her home from them with her gift, and when they had failed to return it sent a message to others that she was not the weak prey they thought her to be.

How had it come to this?

As a child, she hadn't noticed the way that eyes followed her when she went to the market with her mother. She hadn't noticed the looks her mother gave to the merchants when they gave her daughter trinkets and baubles. She hadn't understood why her mother had been so scared when she had wandered off to look at something at another stall. She hadn't understood when her mother wouldn't take her to the market anymore.

When she had tearfully asked her mother why she was being punished her mother had pulled her into her lap and wrapped her arms tight around her.

"No, my darling. You aren't being punished. I'm doing this to protect you," she remembered her mother saying. "One day you will understand, my clever girl, and when you do you will wish you never did." Her mother had murmured into the curls on the top of her head.

She had cried herself to sleep in her mother's arms that night. In her dreams, a grey-eyed woman watched over her with a sorrowful expression.

The next day when her mother came home from the market, she brought a tutor with her. The tutor had given her some puzzles to solve while she spoke with her mother.

It took her no time at all to complete the puzzles and the tutor had smiled when she had asked for more. From that day on when her mother went to the market the tutor came to the house and taught her something new.

The days passed joyfully for her as she soaked up knowledge like a sponge, always eager for more, and she never begged to go with her mother to the market again.

Why won't they leave me alone?

She could hear the intruder's footsteps echo down the stony passages as he moved through her home, determined to find her yet cautious.

He had learned from the fate of the others and came prepared in ways that none of the others ever thought to be. No one had come this far into her home and she wasn't sure how she was going to escape. She knew the tunnels like the back of her hand and had made preparations for the possibility that she might one day have to leave her home, but she had always assumed that it would be at a time of her choosing. Not once had she thought that she would be forced to run in fear from this cold yet comforting home she had made for herself.

The faint illumination that filtered down through cracks in the ceiling had always been more than enough for her to navigate by but in her panic, she had lost track of the turns she had made.

Was she closer to her weapons or a tunnel to the outside? She couldn't go back to check the marks she had left at the last turning; the glow of the intruder's torch was too close for her to chance it. The dancing shadows created by the flame reflecting off his armor made the familiar tunnels feel hostile. Why wouldn't he leave her alone?

Why won't they leave me alone?

As a teenager, she had been flattered by the way the boys had paid attention to her. Every day they would give her little gifts of flowers or sweets, though her mother never let her keep them and would often chase the boys away before they could speak to her.

She hadn't understood why her mother would make her stay in her room when men came to the door. She tried to make friends with the other girls her age but could find nothing in common to talk about. They wanted nothing more than to share the latest gossip or to discuss the latest fashions and gave her strange looks when she talked about politics or commented on the tactical advantages of the army's new uniforms.

She hadn't understood why they called her hateful things after boys approached her with their gifts and she stopped seeking out their company after she heard them call her a devious snake when they thought she couldn't hear them.

A priestess had found her crying under an olive tree and held her as the hot tears ran down her face while she explained what had happened. The woman had dried her tears with the corner of her dress and helped her to stand and dust herself off. The priestess had walked with her back to her home, arriving nearly at sunset to find her mother wrapped in her father's arms in tears.

Her parents had risen at the priestess's entrance with fearful looks in their eyes which cleared when they saw their daughter standing slightly behind her. Her mother had rushed to check her over and only once she was satisfied her daughter was unharmed did she speak to the priestess. Her parents and the priestess had spoken long into the night after she had been sent to her room.

The next day her parents explained that the priestess would be coming back to bring her to the temple of Athena for training.

At first, she had cried thinking that her parents didn't want her anymore but when they explained that the priestess believed finding her under the olive tree was a sign she calmed down.

Later, on the brief journey, the priestess told her about life in the temple and what some of her duties would be. The grey-eyed woman watched over her sleeping form that night with a smile.

Why won't they leave me alone?

From her perch on the stone overhang, she could see all but the tunnel mouth immediately below her. The intruder was relentless in his pursuit of her through the caves, avoiding several pitfalls and traps with ease.

For the first time, she began to wonder if he was more than just another mortal man. He had floated across the top of the last pitfall with ease and since then she hadn't heard his footsteps behind her anymore. She could almost believe he had given up but something in the air told her he was still there. She lay still as a statue for several minutes waiting for him to enter the cavern below her. Her thoughts raced trying to figure out why this man was so stubbornly persistent in his pursuit of her. Many men had hounded her through the years, eventually tiring of the chase or being forced to stop when faced with the power of her gift. There had been only one time she couldn't persuade her pursuer to leave her alone and it had cost her everything. But she was stronger now. She could protect herself now, unlike when she was younger.

Deep in thought, she almost missed it when a snake darted from the tunnel on the right and was silently sliced in two. For just a moment she could make out the bloodstained edge of a sword in the shadows. Her pursuer was there, invisible in the darkness below. She was certain now that there was much more to this man than any of the others. At the very least he was receiving aid from the Gods, and if he was receiving that kind of assistance it was likely that he carried the blood of a God within him. That would explain the persistence as well.

But why would any of the Gods want her dead?

Will I ever be safe?

As a young woman, she had blossomed both in mind and body within the confines of Athena's temple. She understood now why her mother had been so worried about her as a child and teenager. She understood why men and boys had always wanted to give her things, and why the girls had judged her so harshly. She became aware of the hungering stares of men when she would leave the temple with the other priestesses. The feel of their eyes on her body made her blood run cold. More than once she found herself paralyzed by those looks and could only shake free of it when her fellow priestesses surrounded her, veiling her from view.

A man had tried to drag her into an alley once on a market day and she had only escaped with the help of her fellow priestesses. After that, she had begged to be given only duties that kept her within the temple. For the most part, the elder priestesses were able to accommodate her request but there were still some duties that necessitated her leaving the temple from time to time.

To counter her fear of these times she had convinced the temple guards to train her with weapons small enough that she could conceal them in her robes. Armed with her wits and the dagger at her side she had been able to leave the temple with confidence once again. Her confidence acted as a shield against the unwanted attentions of the men outside the temple and the few who weren't deterred were quickly turned away by the blade in her hand.

There was one exception. At first, she had thought him a sailor because of the sea salt smell that seemed to surround him and the rolling way that he walked as if he were unaccustomed to walking on land. She had felt his eyes upon her as she placed offerings at the small shrines to the other Gods in the center of town along with the other priestesses. Then he started coming to the ceremonies at the temple of Athena, it was easy to spot him in the crowd because he stood so much taller than everyone else. There was something in his eyes that she had feared.

Will I ever be safe?
Knowing that the Gods were supporting this latest intruder to her home she began to panic again. There could be no hiding from the Gods. If they were determined that she should die they would find a way to make it happen. She had given up everything to live here away from the eyes of man. She had kept to herself and only used her gift to protect herself.

A prayer to Athena slipped silently from her lips as she crawled through the tiny side passage leading back to the main cavern. With any luck, she could retrieve the few items of meaning to her and escape before the intruder figured out she had doubled back. Her old priestess robe, a few pieces of jewelry, a figure of Athena she had carved from a stone, all remnants of a life she could never live again.

Who was helping this man in his pursuit, she wondered as she gathered her meager treasures. To cross the pitfall in the way he did must mean that he's wearing the winged sandals of Hermes, though how she could have angered the God of Travel she couldn't be sure.

It was clear to her now that the intruder was more than simply good at hiding in the shadows, he had been given the power of invisibility and the most likely source would be Hades' cap of invisibility. She knew of no reason for the God of the Underworld to be angry with her, but if she had angered either of his brothers, she knew he would back them.

She knew from experience that she was no match for a God, especially one of that trio. Not even with the blessing of Athena could she hope to stand against that kind of strength. Once she had thought differently.

Will I ever be safe?

She hadn't understood at first who the sailor really was. Though in hindsight the signs were there. The smell of the sea, the eyes that held the untold depths of the ocean, the way the crowd would flow around him. She should have known this was no mortal man, but a God.

Some would say she should have been flattered to draw the attention of Poseidon. Others would say that she had led him to believe she was interested. In the end, it would be his word against hers. A God against a mortal was no contest.

She had thought herself safe within the temple. Surely no one, not even a God, would dare defile such a sacred space? She had run as fast as she could to the temple and through the courtyard. She could feel his presence behind her surging forward like a tidal wave. In her terror, she didn't notice the absence of the temple guards. Her breath came ragged through her chest as she threw herself down at the base of Athena's altar.

Behind her, the doors of the sanctuary had blown open with the force of a typhoon wind behind them. Her hair whipped around her face in the wind as she watched the God of the Sea stride toward her. She dragged herself upright against the altar to face her pursuer. She felt herself drowning in the depths of his eyes and at that moment, he strode forward and grabbed her. The dagger fell from her hand as he pulled her down behind the altar and took the prize that he desired.

Hot tears fell from her eyes as she stared up into the grey-eyed face of Athena's statue, praying for help that never came.

How had it come to this?

Lost in her memories of that fateful day, Medusa curled up on her bed clinging to the faded priestess robe she had once worn. That life had been taken from her by the actions of Poseidon. When the other Olympians had heard his tale of how she had defiled her Goddess's temple with him they'd demanded that she be punished.

Athena had seen everything and had been powerless to help her priestess. Now the Gods were conspiring to take this new life from her as well.

The Goddess had come to Medusa as she lay battered from the rough attentions of Poseidon and kneeling beside her had lifted the priestess's head into her lap. Athena ran her fingers through the tangled locks of Medusa's long hair as she spoke gently to the priestess.

"My darling, clever Medusa. They will say I am doing this to punish you but know that what I do now is to protect you," she remembered the Goddess murmuring into her hair. She had given Medusa the power to freeze men with her stare the way they had once done to her.

The snakes Athena had made of her locks shifted restlessly as Medusa lay silently weeping on her bed. Her body was so still that the intruder believed her to be sleeping. She was exhausted to the core of her being. She understood now that her life would be nothing but one pursuit after another as it had been one way or another her entire life. She heard the faint hiss of the intruder's sword being drawn as he entered the cave, her home.

She was done running.

Jennifer Woodings

AUTHOR NOTE

Cursed is an alternate take on the classical Greek myth of Medusa.
One version of the myth tells us that Medusa was cursed to be a
Gorgon for the sin of being raped by Poseidon in the temple of
Athena. I was inspired by a post on Tumblr talking about how
Medusa was punished for being a victim that made me think about
how history is written by the winners and often through the male
gaze.

AUTHOR BIOGRAPHY

Jennifer studied English Writing at Edinboro University but was forced to stop before finishing her degree when she was diagnosed with a rare lung disease called Lymphangioleiomyomatosis (LAM). She's always dreamed of being an Author and telling stories that could help people escape reality, if only for a little while. A self-described perfectionist and procrastinator, she knows that someday she's going to be awesome. In the meantime, she's in the process of starting a blog about books and her journey with LAM. This is Jenni's third published short story. Her previous work can be found in *The Second and Third Nine Lives of Squeekie the Bookstore Cat* and *The Very, Very Bad Misadventures of Annika the Reluctant Bookstore Cat.*

Visit her blog at http://fromthebibliophilesattic.blogspot.com
Learn more about LAM at https://www.thelamfoundation.org/

12

Nursery Rhyme for Modern Day

Katie Twigg

There was an old lady who swallowed a cat
She never liked it much for it had a crooked back
She kicked it and beat it and smacked it some more
She broke it down until its will she tore
"You're worthless" she spat "no one wants you around"
Then she picked up a stick and gave it another pound
But no matter how she hit, the cat didn't go away
It whimpered and cried, begging in disarray
"Please I've done nothing, this is just how I look"
"That's why you deserve this" she laughed "and your freedom I took"
Fed up with looking at the crooked cat she grabbed a big cup
Stuffed that cat in and swallowed it right up
Satisfied with being rid of the cat, she cheered in delight
Then shadows appeared on the horizon, in her line of sight
All the cats came, the reds, greens, and blues
All the cats came in their many shapes and hues
They came to fight the old lady against her long oppression
They wouldn't stand for the treatment and arose from depression
They bit and clawed, fed up with her transgressions
But with her whacking stick she beat them into submission
Their momentum they lost preparing for defeat
Their friend was gone but they were plenty used to being beat
They wanted to fight with all their might but she was too big
Then *they* arrived, the dogs, horses, skunks, and pigs
They had seen over the long years the lady's horrid behavior
Not another being would die due to their sad failure
For so long they had stood to the side watching her torture

85

From that day forward, they would be the cats' supporter
The horses attacked high, the skunks attacked low
Even the ducks tried their best with their ducklings in tow
But as much as they hurt her, the lady wouldn't give up
Until she suddenly choked, and felt the welling need to throw up
The crooked back cat sat in her stomach hearing his friends
He didn't want to stop fighting until he met his very end
"They aren't your friends they just pretend" she howled her trickery
"They'll hate your crooked back. I'm helping you out of your misery"
The cat ignored her and tore apart her insides with vicious claws
The others ripped into the lady from the outside without pause
Finally they broke through her tough, withered skin
And the crooked cat emerged wearing a huge grin
He cried and thanked his friends new and old
And away they went from the lady's body, now cold
There had been no hope for survival with the cat on his own
But when they all got together none of them suffered alone
They fought for each other and stood by their sides
When they came together, no one challenged their pride
One may falter and dozens may fail
But when all together, all will prevail

There was an old lady who swallowed a cat
The cat fought back and that was that

AUTHOR NOTE

This piece came together as I watched the current events unfold throughout 2020. Many significant times throughout history have poems or children's songs attached to them. "Ring Around the Rosie" or "Ring a Ring o' Roses" has been determined to be about plagues or the Black Death specifically. "London Bridge is Falling Down" is suspected to be about any number of disasters, but most frequently attributed to the devastating Great Fire of London in 1666. I thought it was time for 2020 to have a nursery rhyme as well.

AUTHOR BIOGRAPHY

Katie Twigg is a Central Pennsylvania native. She is a recent 2020 graduate from Pennsylvania State University with an Associate of Arts Degree in Letters, Arts, and Sciences. Being a long time book lover led her to working at Cupboard Maker Books where she is currently the Community Outreach Coordinator. Katie has several published pieces and won a writing award in high school. When she isn't reading, she takes care of her many plants and pets, five cats and a chinchilla.

13

Evilution

Eric Hardenbrook

Lilly caught movement out of the corner of her eye. She turned and spotted the overturned Styrofoam coffee cup given flight by the wind. Grande sized, of course.

Was there something in that cup? She seemed to recall an article from Sciencey Stuff Monthly that said cups like those wouldn't degrade in a landfill for something close to a thousand years. Her environmental studies instructor, Professor Wilson, didn't like the magazine, but it usually had things broken down into understandable terms.

She had been forced to read more about the environment at her new school. Moving because of something one of your parents had done didn't seem very fair most days, but extra environmental science classes definitely fell into the cruel and unusual punishment category.

But being subjected to paparazzi was the worst. Those guys were always creepy and terrible.

She reached toward the cup, but it swirled away just as she bent down. Wafting breezes shifted and spun through the maze of concrete and glass that was the city where she lived now. The cup tumbled and whirled, skipping toward an alley. She was sure there was something off about this stupid cup.

She grunted and wheezed a little as she tried to walk after the cup while still bent over. Once again it rode a light breeze and hopped beyond her grasp.

She stopped and stood up. She couldn't duck waddle like that. Somebody would see her. Nobody should take pictures from behind you, it was unflattering. It's so embarrassing having people stare at her so much. Her stomach turned a little and she glanced around looking for stray cameramen. She hated dodging them. She could feel her heart rate going up and that just made her huff more. She knew her cheeks would be that awful, blotchy color when she was upset. It just wasn't fair. She wanted to hide.

The cup rolled through the steam coming up from a manhole cover into the deeper shadows of the alley. Lilly hesitated, scanning the street around her. There was a storm coming. Nobody was looking in her direction yet, but she was pretty sure she'd spotted a photographer just down the block.

She was so frustrated. It would be so simple to turn a blind eye and walk away. If somebody did see her ignoring the garbage, she could try claiming she didn't know about the cup. That defense hadn't worked out well in her parents' case. Negligence. Lilly was fairly certain that was one of the terms used in the court papers, but she didn't remember all of it with certainty.

Lilly always thought it looked green right before a big storm, but the colors here were tinted by all the bland buildings surrounding her. The cup tumbled and shifted a few steps away. Glancing back, the person she thought might be a paparazzi was definitely looking her way. She didn't want to go into the alley, but pictures would be worse. Lilly missed her friends. Nobody would walk with her now. She felt very alone these days.

Lilly shook herself. Wasting too much time daydreaming would mean she wouldn't get back to school grounds before it started to rain. Heading into the alley was what she had to do. Just a few short months ago she would have let the cup go, but she realized that it was exactly the sort of thing that would cause her trouble. Once your father gets convicted on illegal dumping charges as the head of a major manufacturing company, people expect you'll follow in his footsteps and are always watching. It was depressing to think of spending the rest of her life making up for somebody else's actions. Her mind was made up. She would just step in, crush the cup so it couldn't blow any further along, then pick it up and toss it in a nearby trash can. Simple.

Lilly stepped into the gloom between the bank tower and the local franchise of Frank's Franks. As she brought her foot down to smash the cup it turned end for end and showed her a tiny man inside the cup.

Lilly swung her foot wide, stumbled, and narrowly avoided smashing the offending cup and miniature man within.

She staggered against the edge of a dumpster, regaining her balance. She raised her hands to rub her eyes, then realized her hand had been on a very unsanitary dumpster, in an alley, next to a chain restaurant. She used the heels of her hands and rubbed her eyes anyway. Opening her eyes again showed her the tiny man she had seen hiding inside the blowing cup was still there. She was thunderstruck.

He had iridescent wings that were folded down against his back. The ends were rounded and she could see the tiny veins that extended into them. His features were narrow and sharp, jutting out from beneath a tuft of wild green hair.

He looked... she wanted to say it, but it didn't seem right. He looked like a fairy. Sort of a cross between Tinker Bell and a pirate captain from the movies. She had a small collection of fairy books in her room and had always enjoyed the images. Adding a pirate to the mix didn't seem to fit with any of those images. She couldn't recall any fairies being dressed, never mind having little scrap leather boots and a tarnished charm bracelet sash. The rest of his outfit was a miss-mash of rags and string.

The diminutive man's eyes widened as he realized she had seen him. In a flash he heaved his feet out of the cup and dashed for cover behind the dumpster.

Lilly's body was still catching up to her mind. She had just encountered the single most amazing thing in all of her life, and she stood there dumbfounded while he ran away.

She jerked into motion just as the minuscule man moved out of sight. Errant cup forgotten, she dashed further into the alley. Scanning left and right she attempted to track down the fairy. The alley contained mounds of garbage bags, forming a short series of rolling hills. Broken pallets stood on end here and there, looking like tree trunks leaning back into the gloom. Tattered newspaper hung here and there giving the impression of leaves with discarded plastic strapping dangling like vines. In the briefest of moments, the random collection of items he wore had helped him blend into the piles of garbage bags and other random bits of refuse. She took a few steps further, calling out hesitantly, "Hello?"

Suddenly movement erupted all around her. She wanted, needed, tried, to scream in fright, but her throat only managed a short-lived 'eek'.

She now stood at the center of a circle composed of garbage bags, mold, and even a few tiny mushrooms that had managed to grow in the damp and dark of the alley.

In front of her, blocking her view of the street beyond was another, much larger being. He was almost her size. He had wings made of plastic garbage bags and old wire coat hangers. His head was covered not in hair, but in a fine coating of fungus that looked remarkably like the stuff growing in the alley. He carried a broken chair leg in one hand and a plastic trash can lid held like a shield in the other. His torso was wrapped toga style with a discarded sofa cover judging by the large flower pattern. He had strapped broken wooden planks to his shins. This quasi gladiator shuffled forward and waved the chair leg at her. She could see the rusty, bent nails protruding from the end.

She glanced to her left and saw more fairy folk – they couldn't be anything else. Garbage fairies. There was a short, fat little one that looked as though he had the wings of a fly. His head was covered with a plastic fireman's helmet with chicken bones protruding from it Viking style. The effect would have been comical, but she then noticed the fur cape it wore still had the rat's head attached. The fireman Viking wielded a bent metal fork with sharpened tines.

There was another menacing little fey that had poked her arms and head through a discarded plastic shopping bag and wore it like a dress. Flowing mustard colored hair held back in a ponytail bound with bread ties was accentuated by dark streaks of black soot used as makeup. The look was accessorized with a piece of broken mirror taped to the end of a shish kebab skewer.

Lilly spun around and found her retreat blocked by a pair of tiny folk riding squirrels. Each of the riders wore plastic doll boots and plastic soldier style camouflage helmets. They held cut off straws in one hand and the reins of their mounts in the other. Both wore a sash holding needles bandolier style. The squirrels were mangy and their eyes glowed red. Little bits of foam dripped from the corners of their mouths.

Lilly twisted around again and spotted the tiny man that had led her astray. He now stood on a stack of overturned milk crates. The crates resembled a finger of rock jutting from the side of a worn hill. His head almost reached her shoulder height from that vantage point. He had added a silver foil crown, a long cape, and toothbrush scepter topped with a ring pop to his previous outfit of rags and dirt stained charms.

"Woe to you human! Your waste and wanton destruction shall bring ruin down upon your head!"

The thunderstorm that had been brewing made itself known with a low rumble. The tiny leader's voice seemed louder than it should have in the alley.

"We shall rain destruction down upon you and all your wicked kind!"

He gestured toward his companions to emphasize their presence. They all shifted and began to circle her, never entering the ring of mushrooms she stood in.

"The land may no longer be completely ours, but this war is far from over. The true battle has yet to begin. We will adapt to your ways. We will change and learn and grow. We will discover the way to defeat you once and for all!"

Lilly stared at this tiny creature in disbelief. She couldn't begin to imagine what in the world he meant. She uttered the most articulate response she could muster.

"Huh?"

The leader's eyes widened as his face turned a vivid shade of purple.

"Do not mock me! I will rally many more followers. I will add to my numbers with bridge trolls large enough to eat one of your horseless metal carts."

Lilly could hear the distant blowing of car horns.

"I will reshape your barrels of poisonous waste into a mighty fortress. The animals and birds you have tried to destroy will adapt and learn new ways to survive in your lands of stone and glass and become our mighty steeds!"

Rain began to fall in fat, plopping drops. The fairy prince used his free hand to pull his cloak of pigeon feathers up over his shoulder.

"Even now we live and move among your kind. We dash across your rivers of black stone disguised as blowing wrappers or cups. You see us everywhere from the corner of your vision, yet we slide easily away. Our squirrel mounts climb your wires and scratch openings into your homes. We surround you, and are never seen."

Lilly tried to connect her brain to her mouth again,

"You're going to what? I must be going insane." She wrinkled her brow.

This was not the vision she had of fairies. Fairies were whimsical and fun loving creatures living in the wild areas of the world. The forests and fields where fireflies could be seen at twilight.

These were angry, dangerous looking creatures despite their miniature stature. She decided she was getting out of there.

Turning back toward the street she had come in from she tried to step over the rabid looking squirrel riders. Her foot caught on something and she tripped forward. Before she could fall to the ground, potentially squishing the rodent wranglers, her nose smacked into something as hard as a concrete wall. The rest of her weight followed her into this barrier and she jammed the middle finger of her right hand as she tried to catch herself.

She rebounded from this invisible wall, stumbled, and fell backward, flat on her backside. The ring of garbage and fungus sizzled and glistened. The circle was the base of a wall of force swirling to life around her. It took on the look of a slick in a puddle that rippled where she had banged into it. An oily rainbow spun and whirled in her vision.

"Stupid girl! Did you think we lack power because there are no longer any trees? We have changed. We have grown in strength despite our dwindling numbers. We now control all the spaces you don't wish to inhabit. We live in the world you have made and we will be feared again! Strike her now, my warrior!"

He motioned toward her with a wave of his scepter. Lilly turned her head around in time to see one of the fairy folks was actually inside the circle with her.

He had been laying still along the edges of some mushrooms. He had the same weapon as the squirrel riders. He dipped a wicked needle tip into a vaguely purple and green slime that was seeping from a split garbage bag. This needle had been taped to half of an ear swab, not like the smaller, sharper looking ones strung in the bandoleers of the riders.

The inside warrior pushed his makeshift dart into his cut off straw and crammed the fluffy end of the swab in behind. Only when he raised the straw to his lips and puffed out his cheeks did it occur to Lilly what he intended – a blowgun.

She squeaked again, throwing her arm up to protect her face. She heard a wheezing puff of breath as the warrior let fly the tainted ammunition. Lilly felt the hodgepodge dart jab into her armpit. He puffed again and another jabbed her in the side of her neck, away from the cover of her arm.

She yelped in pain. The needles stung and the skin started to tingle almost immediately. She pulled her other arm up to remove the offending stickers and rolled onto her knees. As she did the sharp odor of rotting eggs assailed her. Her eyes began to water and her nose began to run and she was suddenly, terribly dizzy.

Flopping onto her side she found herself staring into the face of the fat fireman Viking. He was chewing on what looked like a chunk of mottled green eggshell and had a hand in a bag at his side. As she struggled to get back up on her knees, he laughed and did an odd little dance. The inside warrior had approached closer than Lilly realized. He dipped a hand into his own bag. When he whipped his hand out he tossed some kind of dust into the air. A deep breath of fear was her natural reaction and the worst thing she could have done.

She got a mouthful of foul, sharp bits. Some of the bits landed in her right eye. She immediately closed her eyes and began trying to spit the debris out of her mouth. She had managed to raise herself to her knees again, but now curled back toward the ground to spit again and again.

The rain that had started slowly was now pouring down and proved to be her saving grace. She scooped up some of the water that had gathered in a puddle within her circle and splashed some into her mouth. She gagged as rust flavor battled the other putrescence in her impromptu mouthwash.

She retched, and retched again, finally managing to vomit. She heard a ragged cheer from the crowd surrounding her. She tried to focus on her situation and find a way out. Squinting her left eye, she could just see past the armored legs of the largest of the garbage fairies. The alley they had chosen for this elaborate ambush sloped from one end to the other. A large flow of storm runoff was winding its way down the alley carrying more litter.

Squinting as she was, the colors of the alley mixed with the rain almost gave her the impression of a river flowing through a peaceful valley. She imagined the sounds of songbirds and the gurgle of a fast flowing stream. The flow was headed directly toward her.

Lilly recalled from one of the movies she had seen that a witch's circle only worked if it was complete and unbroken. The fairies must be using the circle of mushrooms as a magical means of holding her. A flotilla of trash rode the rainwater runoff. It looked to smash through the circle that held her. The storm would be her rescue. All she needed was to keep the fey focused on her, rather than the impending breach of their circle.

She touched the area where the needle had struck her neck. It was already swelling. She could feel a painful burning sensation running along the muscle of her shoulder. Glaring at the leader from her good eye, she yelled. It was inarticulate but had the desired effect. The fey folk laughed and hissed at her rage.

She gathered her feet beneath herself and waited for the flow to reach her. Another needle jab struck her in the back. Lightning flashed just as the wave of trash hit the edge of the circle. A wrapper from Frank's Franks and a losing lottery ticket stub slid in first. The swirling, oily barrier flickered and fell. She felt the release snap and a pressure she hadn't noticed lifted.

Lilly launched herself at the largest of her foes. The fairies wailed as her attack hit home unexpectedly. The circle no longer contained her. Lilly crushed one of the garbage bag wings as she crashed into the improvised shield and knocked the dirty sprite into a heap of fruit crates. Coughing and staggering she made her way toward the street at the end of the alley as quickly as she could. Shrieks of rage and venom followed her, sounding like the angry wind of the storm pushing out of the narrow passage between buildings.

Moving at a stumbling run, Lilly started back toward the school grounds. She needed to get clean and dry. Her right eye was still blurry and felt as though there were something pointy floating around in it, scraping each time she looked in a new direction. The swelling from the needle shots had reached an alarming size already and she could feel an unwelcome warmth flowing from the shot in her armpit.

She jumped and yelped in fear again as she reached one of the city's many public waste receptacles. Just as she had staggered beyond the can a Styrofoam cup skittered past. She wasn't sure if it was her imagination working overtime or if the fairy leader had really been rolling past in the cup. She spit a mouthful of metallic tasting blood and sharpened debris onto the sidewalk.

Lilly needed help, and she needed it fast. If only she could come up with something that wouldn't make her sound crazy. Where were all those stupid camera people now? Ran for shelter from the rain of course. If she tried to tell anyone about her plight they would say she had obviously gone mad under the stress of dealing with all the attention after her father's conviction. She needed something, but it had to be believable. Angry fairies were only going to get her sent for therapy and extra medicine.

Lilly rounded the last corner before her school grounds. Her arm was going numb. It was becoming more and more difficult to breathe.

She jumped when a garbage bag slid sideways down a wet pile near the curb. She could hear the squealing air brakes and whine of the compressor of a garbage truck in the distance.

Where did all the regular garbage go? How much did people cram into landfills each and every day? She supposed it was far too much. Her mind was wandering and her vision began to blur. Why couldn't she focus? The world was starting to spin. The only other time she had experienced a feeling like this was when she had been ushered out of a court building through the middle of a massive, angry crowd. The sheer number of screaming, angry people had overwhelmed her.

That sparked the idea she needed. She'd go to the environmentalists. Somebody there would know about fairies. She was sure of it.

She knew they would believe her, and the possibility that it would make her parents want to move again was an added bonus. She wasn't sure what her claim would do for the cause of environmentalists, but that was something she'd consider later.

She didn't feel like walking anymore. She wanted to sit and consider the environment and the impact people had on it.

The school's security guard had seen her and was already running in her direction. She saw him raising his radio to call in when everything shifted. She was laying down on the sidewalk and staring at the clouds. The sidewalk was cold, but she didn't mind. The wet of the rain didn't really matter at all.

The wind shrieked and swirled.

"We'll get you," she swore she heard the fairy prince's squeaking voice fading in the wind, "You're helping us now."

Her vision darkened down to a tunnel, reminding her of the alley.

"You can't hide."

It was difficult to breathe.

"We're behind the shed, we're under a pile of bags or we're riding the wind with a waxy sail and we'll get you all one day!"

AUTHOR BIOGRAPHY

Eric is a fan, an author and an artist, usually in that order. Eric lives in central Pennsylvania with his gorgeous wife and daughter. He writes to try to get the stories out of his head. When he's being a fan he helps run <u>Watch The Skies</u> and assists in the publication of their monthly fanzine. He can be found (at least some of the time) at <u>The Pretend Blog</u>. When not working on those things, Eric enjoys the board game and is an old school role player, occasionally appearing as a guest on <u>Attacks of Opportunity</u>.

14

Clockwork

Samantha Coons

The rush of the fractions halted in tandem as the minute hand ground one tick closer over the horizon with a mechanical shudder that left the ivory streets beneath Umbra's feet groaning. The grinding and gnawing of the gears beneath the city washed into the stillness left by the roar of the hand.

None of the crowd spoke, but all stayed perfectly still a beat longer with every face turned to the looming darkness of the hand. Then eyes shifted nervously.

Move, move, move.... Umbra repeated in her head. She glared not at the hand, but at the crush of microseconds and nanoseconds around her. Vibrations gripped her whole body in fierce waves. None of the nanos around her turned to look at her, no one noticed. But still they grew worse within her with every tick.

A pop sounded behind her, and she knew another nano had disappeared. As quickly and surely as a bubble bursting.

Another pop to her left, and several to her right, and the crowd began buzzing.

MOVE.

A microsecond in front of her turned with narrowed eyes and she realized she was chanting her thoughts out loud. She pressed her mouth closed and the micro kept walking. She slowed until a respectable gap lay between her and the stranger.

"It's a wonder the hands aren't moving *slower*," she muttered to herself, "If everyone keeps stopping to gawk every tick."

She spotted the huddled nanos ahead of her and dread pulsed through her. She kept her eyes forward but still caught a glance at the poor fraction amid the gathered onlookers. Pale and flickering wildly, slumped on the ground where they had stood at the tick.

The other nanos would collect these stalled nanos and take them out of the way. Where she didn't know. She didn't want to know.

What she knew was the vibrations inside her weren't good, and if, at the next tick, she slumped to the ground to stall into eternity or popped out of existence entirely then she might as well get some answers first.

If this was a Quicken, if the clock was speeding up, then there had to be an answer.

There had to be.

Umbra forced down the impulse to spit on the street. Nanos had been disappearing for twelve-hours, thousands by now. One more was nothing – *she* was nothing. But still she turned down a slender alley heading numberwise.

Umbra kept her head down through the taller structures marking the microseconds territory. Nanos travelled through this area constantly with deliveries or other menial business · but better to be careful then to risk being caught poking her nose around.

The smooth white ivory of the towers stretched farther into the sky with every street numberwise. Now milliseconds strode along with purpose, a few raising a brow at her as she hurried past.

Milliseconds flickered less than herself and the other nanos. She grew used to rhythmic strobe of the microseconds over the years but the gentle strum of milliseconds sent a fresh wave of vibrations through her. She kept her eyes down for her own comfort as much as to keep a low profile.

Umbra switched tactics as she climbed the ramp into the seat of the 24th Second. She strode through the archway into the Second's Timepiece with her chin jutting up and her shoulders wide, as if she had every right to go wherever she pleased.

The minute hand loomed overhead, only three ticks away, and the milliseconds bustled about their preparations for its arrival. Micros sped every which way as the millis snapped out their orders.

The chaos of the impending ticks provided the smokescreen Umbra needed, practically invisible as she marched up the spiraling ramp leading to the Second's workshop.

If anyone thought it strange that a nano wandered around the Timepiece, panicked efficiency smothered their surprise. No one said as much as a word to her.

Even the Second didn't look up from his cranks and dials when she came to halt before him.

He flickered in a slow pulse, nearly solid. She raised her chin a little higher as the vibrations rocked through her again.

She folded her arms.

He tapped a meter then shuffled a step to the right. He glanced at her as he spun a dial.

"Your message, quick now. Fractions are waiting on these measurements," he snapped.

Umbra grit her teeth as the fit of vibrations ended on a rattling tremor that almost sent her to her knees.

"The clock is speeding up."

The Second didn't pause in his frantic work, didn't even blink.

"Fluctuations happen, nothing more than a few nanoseconds here and there. But the clock doesn't speed up. Everything is balanced."

She kept her arms folded. The conviction in his voice may have swayed her if the memory of the vibrations didn't still rattle through her bones.

The Second peered down at her, his solidness fading for a few flickers before shifting back.

"A nano, aren't you? If there is a problem, the Seconds and Minutes will know before you."

He dismissed her with a hasty wave of a hand.

Umbra felt the argument bubble up from her gut but she quelled it before it burst from her mouth. She swallowed before spinning to stomp out of the Timepiece. The Second far too busy with his measurements to heed the likes of her.

Back on the ivory pathways, she vented her frustration on passing millis and micros.

"The clock is speeding up," she barked.

The millis barely took a flicker to stare down their noses at her. Most of the micros at least paused to look shifty and mutter about the higher units before scuttling away from her.

One micro froze in their tracks to level a stare at her.

"The Hour would tell us about something like a Quicken. You and the other nanos need to stay dialwise, and keep busy. Obviously you need more work if your imaginations are throwing you into a panic."

They left her with a sneer and Umbra barely managed to squash the urge to kick them in the rear.

At a nearby crossroads a handful of millis clustered together, muttering and shooting her glances. She clenched her fists and forced herself to move farther numberwise.

She passed the Second's mark proper, not stopping until she came to the Gears access gate.

She threw her shoulder into it. The solid metal didn't even have the good grace to squeak. She launched herself into it again without any more success.

A vibration sent her to her knees. The hour hand hadn't moved yet, but it wouldn't be long. Her throat closed up at the thought of another tick. She struggled to her knees and pounded the gate with her fists.

The gate groaned and jolted open a crack.

Umbra blinked and dragged herself to her feet before she realized voices approached from the other side. She tripped over her feet as she sprinted to hide down a side street, just out of view.

The voices swelled and she inched forward until she could see the open gates. A few Cogs walked past, joking with each other. She waited until they just slid out of sight into the path leading to the Timepiece before rushing to the gate as it began to grind shut.

She kept her feet soft and she made it through without attracting attention. Out of time to ponder her lunacy, she consulted a map posted on the wall. A gear-room lay just beneath her, only a few turns.

The grind of teeth reached her before she came out into the vast space filled with metal of all kinds of shapes and sizes, all slotted together in a deafening dance.

She felt her vibrations began anew, and only after a moment did she realize that it was not her vibrations at all but rather the linked network of gears shuddering through her.

Stationed nearby, a Cog held a can of oil. Her steps shook as she approached.

"The clock is going faster," she said through chattering teeth.

The Cog wrinkled her nose and jerked away from Umbra.

"I think not," she growled.

She moved toward another Cog down the way but Umbra grabbed ahold of her arm.

"Please, something must be done."

She felt faint. The tick was coming.

The Cog spat on the ground.

"I've done things the same way since the clock was brand new. Nothing moves faster or slower. Now get out."

She left Umbra standing there with the shudder of the gears. Umbra looked up at the gears grinding above her head. She saw the patches of flaking metal at the axels.

She stumbled to the next Cog and pointed up at the rust.

"Something has to be done," she insisted.

This Cog looked sympathetic, at least. Did that mean something? Her head hurt from her vibrations layering over the movement of the gears. She didn't know anything.

"We know what we're doing. You, poor thing, need to get back dialwise. This is no place for nanoseconds."

Umbra grit her teeth and moved forward, leaving the Cog shaking their head behind her.

She lurched from Cog to Cog, and all of them knew what they were doing. They knew. And what did she know. She fell to the ground at the other end of the room and looked at her shaking fingers. She didn't see them anymore.

The map of the Gears sprang into her head and she remembered Mainspring in large red letters at the very heart of the clock.

How long would it take to convince the Cogs, the Millis, the Seconds, Minutes, Hours that there was a problem? Who would want to fix something that only hurt Nanos?

She grabbed a long piece of twisted metal from a scrap heap near the door, and mentally pictured the path to the Mainspring.

Maybe there was one thing a nano could still do in less than a tick.

AUTHOR NOTE

What does a modern day fairy tale look like?

Urban fantasy springs to mind, as well as the plethora of fairy tale retellings and re-imaginings. I wanted to try something a little different, go a little more surreal – if you can even call this surreal. The first image I saw was the first image in the story, the giant hand of the clock coming over the horizon. Clocks are ubiquitous in the modern world in one form or another, even if analog clocks like this one are mostly the domain of schoolrooms.

What would a digital clock look like to Umbra?

AUTHOR BIOGRAPHY

Samantha Coons writes words sometimes and sometimes they are even good. She edited this book and wrote any text not attributed to another author. She would like you to know all mistakes in this book are her fault.

15

The Lady of the Lake

Jelaina Jones

I lay on the bottom of the silty lakebed, my hair streaming out around me like tendrils of kelp as I stared up through the murky depths toward the faint glimmer I knew to be the sunlight, and contemplated life.

Well, afterlife, if you're gonna get technical about it, all six-hundred years of it. Six hundred years of haunting these grounds, waiting for the day when my true love would save me from my curse. I didn't have high hopes that today would be that day, but a ghost could dream right?

So how did I wind up as a ghost, contemplating the afterlife at the bottom of a lake? Well, don't most stories of woe begin with a man? Mine certainly does.

Dermot McCarthy was King of Munster, yes, like the cheese. His wife was a meek, sickly little thing who was also mute. While many men of the age wouldn't have minded a mute wife, Dermot wasn't one of them. And so, he sought me out, a witch of some renown, hoping I could cast a spell to cure her. After all, here she was, married to the man who outsmarted the Queen of England with his silver tongue, thus coining the term, "what a bunch of Blarney," and she couldn't utter a syllable. And oh, the things Dermot could do with that tongue. The way he could... uh, never mind.

Dermot and I grew ever closer as I worked to restore his wife's speech. He came to respect me for my talents as spellcaster and herbalist, and also as an excellent conversationalist. I could match him, tit for tat, and we spent many evenings in verbal sparring matches. Everything was perfect. He even planted a yew tree in my honor. As a matter of fact, it won "Tree of the Year" in Ireland in

2019. Yep. You read that correctly. Any excuse to party for us Irish, huh?

Oh, you thought this was a story set in Wales because it's called Lady of the Lake? Like the sword-wielding maiden who bestowed Excalibur on Arthur? Sorry, but no, this story is set at Blarney Castle in Ireland, home of the famous Blarney stone. People have been coming here for years to kiss it, a bluish bit of limestone no one would be kissing if they knew the real story of the nasty thing. Yet, thousands had visited, having heard the rumor that any who kissed the stone would receive the gift of eloquence. A rumor, as it happens, that had all started with me.

Today was no exception. Tour buses soon began pouring in for the day, no doubt laden with tourists eager to play tonsil hockey with a rock. Heaving a sigh, I allowed myself to float up, breaking the surface of the lake…well, metaphorically speaking.

Drifting over to the entrance of the castle, I stopped next to a large group of college students standing around their guide as he incorrectly expounded the story of the stone.

No one knows the true story of the stone. Well, no one alive anyway. There's all kinds of conjecture of course: It was part of the Chair of Kings. That it was the stone of Jacob from the book of Genesis. Reality is that it was just a stone Dermot had lying around after he demolished the first castle and built the one tourists see today. It was the stone I had used as part of my spell, a conduit in my attempts to restore Dermot's wife's speech, and also, in a twisted sense of irony, the stone Dermot later used to drown and curse me.

I told you no one would want to kiss it if they knew the real story. When my body finally floated to the top of the lake, bloated and rotten, with the fleshiest bits of me eaten away by fish, I was scooped out and unceremoniously dumped into a shallow unmarked grave on the grounds. The stone was retrieved by a magician, summoned to the surface and presented to Dermot as a gift. By then, the delayed effect of the spell had restored Dermot's wife speech but I was already dead, cursed for eternity to seek out one of Dermot's blood who might someday restore me to my corporeal body.

I stood, well, not stood exactly, but… confound it, this is annoying. I 'stood' there, the drone of the guide fading away as my eyes slowly worked their way around the group. I dismissed the unfortunate twenty-something that, in addition to gaining the freshman fifteen, hadn't yet grown out of puberty and left his acne in his teen years. It would be a cruel twist of fate if he were the proverbial 'one,' wouldn't it? Surely I would know if he were Dermot's long-lost descendant. I would certainly be able to pick that man out of a crowd, right?

As the tour guide continued to botch the stone's history, I mused over what had actually happened. To cure Dermot's wife, I instructed her to kiss the stone every day for a year hoping the power I had funneled into it through cantrips and incantations would take effect. I had not, however, told her to tongue the thing like a hormonal teenager on her first unchaperoned date. When her chamber maid witnessed the display and set the whole castle to gossip, Dermot had been furious. When the year and a day timeframe came and went with no change, Dermot had flown into a rage, calling me a charlatan and a whore. He accused me of witchcraft and plopped me in the lake. Two weeks later, his wife began speaking.

Many folks around the county begged to be allowed to kiss the stone after his wife's miraculous cure, hoping it would grant their wildest wishes. Dermot soon tired of entertaining people's foolish notions and began telling everyone that the stone's true power was the gift of eloquence, not to grant wishes arbitrarily. After that pronouncement, visitors declined quickly. Apparently, eloquence was not as sought after as say, kingly wealth. The legend, however, stuck, and throughout the years, slowly gained in notoriety, bringing people from all over to seek out the stone. Fools, all of them. And yet, day after day I greeted them, silently observing them, longing for the day when I might find the one who could release me.

I ran a hand through my long, once auburn tresses. Interestingly enough, ghosts don't see in color, though I distinctly remember having flaming red hair, long and luscious. I switched my gaze from the unfortunate acne-plagued soul, and was about to turn my attention to the tall, gangly boy beside him, when suddenly my gaze was drawn to a girl, half hidden behind pox-boy. Sorry, I know that's not nice, but how else would you describe him?

She stood, listening intently to the guide, her hair plaited down the center of her head, the tail of the braid coming to rest over her heart. I didn't need color vision to tell it was black, dark and thick as a raven's tail. She had striking eyes, shrewd and shiny and clear. And though she held herself like a queen, stately and regal in an unassuming way, there was a softness about her that captivated me. There was something strangely familiar about her, from her not quite aquiline nose, to the full lips and laugh lines that had already begun to form around her eyes and mouth. It unsettled me in a way nothing else had.

Pulled toward her like a magnet, I inched closer, until I was hovering directly in front of her. I narrowed my eyes, scrunching up my face unflatteringly, as I tried to wrangle my sense of deja'vu. The young woman started and whipped her head around to glare at the guy next to her.

"Don't touch me!"

The guy's mouth dropped open in surprise. "I, I – didn't," he stammered.

I gasped in shock. It was true. He hadn't touched her. Without realizing it, I had involuntarily reached out to touch her braid. And this woman had actually sensed me. For the first time in over six hundred years, I had made a connection with a living, breathing person.

Mind reeling, I fled to the safety of my Yew tree. What had Dermot said when he cursed me? I struggled to remember his atrocious attempt at a curse. The man may have been loquacious to a fault, but a bard and poet he was not. He couldn't rhyme a couplet to save his life, but in the end managed well enough to take mine.

"Foul witch a curse upon thee,
Bound forever, to this yew tree.
Cursed forever with this stone,
Till one of my blood calls you home.
Cursed are thee to search to find
One of my beloved's and of mine
A kiss from my blood breaks the spell
To raise you from your wat'ry hell."

112

And then he threw me into the lake, the bastard. Subjected me to a horrible rhyme, tied a stone to my ankles, and let it drag me down into the frigid gray water of the lake.

I shook my head to clear it, growling as I failed to keep thoughts of that night away. My chest tightened, breath coming in gasps and I squeezed my eyes shut, willing my mind to think of anything other than my own death. After a while, my breathing slowed, and I was able to regain composure. No, I don't need to breathe, but old habits die hard, alright?

Dermot, terrified of the curse being broken while he was still alive for me to exact revenge, ordered the stone built into an almost inaccessible place in the castle wall, and forbidding all of his blood from seeking it out. Meanwhile, I floated around in limbo, waiting for Dermot's ancestor to pucker up. Where's the justice here?

In all my years roaming the estate looking for the one I thought could break the spell, never once had I thought that the curse might mean I was to look for a woman. Hey now, don't look at me like that! I'm technically over six hundred years old, I think I have a right to be a little old fashioned! Then again, the curse just said, one of my blood. Huh.

Deciding I had better get up to the stone, pronto I pictured it, and a moment later, I was there, floating beside it.

When a Blarney staff member motioned the dark-haired beauty that had so unsettled me over to the stone, excitement built within me. She settled onto her back, reaching out to grasp the metal bars bolted into the wall. Here goes nothing I thought, gliding forward, passing through the solid wall of stone as easily as air. Positioning myself so that my lips would be level with the slight indentation where all the tourists aimed for, I closed my eyes and waited.

And waited. A cheer went up from the woman's friends, and I opened my eyes to see the girl sliding back from the stone and pushing herself up to a standing position.

A bitter sense of disappointment washed over me. I had really thought this time would be different. That she was different. I wanted to cry. I wanted to scream. I wanted to...

I wanted to throw up.

Pain lanced through me and my stomach heaved. I gasped, feeling as though my lungs were trying to expand for the first time in centuries, as if breathing wasn't just a reflex anymore. The edges of my vision began to darken as I fought to stay conscious, my body spasming with the need for oxygen. Eventually, I lost the battle and my vision faded to black.

I awoke to the strangest sensation, as if I could actually feel the sun on my face and the wind caressing my body.

I lay in a thicket, partially concealed by thick brush, some of which was currently digging into my back and nether regions. Wincing, I stared upward, blinking in the bright light as I looked around. A canopy of mottled brown branches and leafy tufts grew wild and tangled above me like... wait. Green. Brown. Logically I know leaves are green and branches are brown, but I hadn't seen those colors in half a millennium.

Heart hammering, I thrust my hand in front of me, marveling at the pinkness of my skin, and the opaque tips of my nails. Shakily, I reached out and crushed a glossy green leaf between thumb and forefinger, the feel of it waxy, the smell sharp and pungent and earthy. Still unable to believe that I was really alive, I did the one thing I knew could convince me.

"Ouch!" I said, pinching myself and immediately rubbing the now tender spot on my arm.

"Uh, hello?"

I glanced down and groaned. Great. I was naked, in a well trafficked tourist spot, with no idea what to do next. And now, I'd been found.

Popping my head out from the thicket, my heart leapt into my throat as I saw her. She was even more beautiful than I had originally thought, the lush lips I had noticed earlier, painted a deep red, a striking contrast with her lightly tanned skin. Her eyes, so bright and captivating when in shades of gray, turned out to be as green as peat moss and were currently assessing me with a curious and amused gaze.

I had to come up with something to explain my strange state, and quickly.

"Hi."

Okay, so it wasn't my most impressive opening line.

"Not that it's any of my business, but you do know you're currently sitting in the middle of a patch of poison ivy, naked, right?"

Just. My. Luck. Thank you so much Dermot, you ungrateful ass.

"Uh. Yes. I was aware of that. You see, I, uh..." I trailed off, grasping for some reason as to why I might be out here, naked as the day I was born.

"You're... hedging." The woman paused between the first and second word, her lips pulling up as she fought to keep from smiling, allowing my brain to catch up.

"Did you really just make a pun at my expense?" I asked, incredulous. "Aren't I already compromised enough?"

"Well, maybe," she conceded, laughing, "but then again, you still haven't told me why you're naked in a briar patch. Not that I mind." Her gaze flicked quickly down, and I realized that I had stood up at some point during our conversation, my bare breasts now exposed for her to see. I sat back down quickly, a flush rising to my cheeks.

"Well, I certainly didn't plan for this to happen," I snapped. "Tell you what. If you find me some clothes, I'll trade you for the story of how I came to be naked and laying in a patch of brambles. Fair?"

The girl gave me a dubious glance, but I could tell she was interested. With a nod, she slung the backpack from her shoulders, and opened it. After rummaging around for several seconds, she produced a short sleeved blue flannel and a pair of jeans.

"This is the best I've got." She said, tossing them at me.

I caught them, grateful, while being careful not to expose myself any further as I crouched behind the thicket.

I thrust one arm into the shirt, a bit big, but that was just fine. "How can I thank you..." I trailed off, realizing that I didn't know her name.

"Carolina."

I stood up, shirt now buttoned, and began to pull the jeans up. They settled nicely on my waist as I zipped them. Fully clothed, albeit barefoot, I stepped out from behind my screen of leaves and nodded.

"I thank you then, Carolina, for assisting me."

Carolina placed her hands on her hips and arched one perfectly shaped eyebrow. "You still owe me a story."

"Yes. I do don't I. Will you walk with me?" Without giving her time to answer, I linked my arm through hers, reveling in the feel of her skin against mine. She glanced at me sideways, but allowed me to lead her along the path, bathed in beams of sunlight and shadow.

Walking arm in arm, I began the story I had formulated while dressing. "I am one of the last practicing druid priestesses in Ireland, descended from an ancient line of witches. Every year the women descended from this ancient line gather here, to pay homage to the one who was slain."

"You mean the Blarney witch?" Carolina inclined her head, turning to look at me questioningly.

"Indeed. She was a fair woman, who was treated unfairly by her lover, Dermot McCarthy. In exchange for healing his wife, Dermot had this witch drowned, as much to get rid of her, as to silence the only person who could have revealed his indiscretion. For you see, he and this witch had been lovers."

"Okay, so that still doesn't tell me how you wound up naked in a briar patch." Carolina smiled, and I felt my lips part in an answering grin.

"Every year, as I said, we travel here and remember her. This year was special, as the anniversary of her death fell on a full moon. On those years, we perform a sacred ritual. While the intricacies of the ritual are secret, I can tell you that in order to perform the ritual, we must first strip off all worldly possessions, and submerge ourselves in the lake." I grimaced. "After completing the ritual, we all shared some of Agatha's homemade Poitín, and well, I'm afraid I may have overindulged. I'm guessing some of the girls thought it would be amusing to hide my clothes and leave me here, hence how you found me just now."

Carolina stopped, and turned to look at me, a look of skepticism on her face. I could tell she wasn't sure whether or not to believe me, so I just smiled, shrugged and sat down on a gnarled tree root that had forced its way up from the ground.

"What a bunch of Blarney." She sat down next to me.

Our shoulders just barely touched. After a moment, she reached out, self-assured and without a second's hesitation, to pull my chin around so that we faced one another. Her eyes narrowed as she stared, her emerald gaze holding my flinty gray one. My breath hitched as she leaned in and I could feel her hot breath as she sighed. My lips parted and I leaned forward, my lips brushing hers. For a second she froze, and then she was kissing me, hot and fervent, our tongues clashing in a frenzy as desire coursed through me. I had never felt so alive.

When I felt as though I might drown for a second time, I broke away, panting and breathless. I glanced at Carolina, the bright red of her lips smudged, her face flushed, her eyes smoldering. I reached out and tucked a loose strand of hair behind her ear and I felt her shiver at the touch. Our eyes met, and for a moment, the world felt as if it had stopped. Then she broke into a grin, laughter bubbling up and bursting forth. In a moment, I was laughing too. She fell against me, and I embraced her, our bodies fitting together in a perfect symmetry. We stayed that way for some time, until with a sigh, Carolina sat up and began rummaging around in her bag.

She pulled out a pen and a notebook, hastily scribbling something down. Then tearing the paper out, she stuffed the pen and book back into her bag and stood.

"I've gotta get back. Our tour bus will be leaving soon. But I want you to have this." She thrust the paper out to me, and on it, framed in a heart, was a number. "I don't give out my phone number to just anyone. So make sure you call me, okay?"

I smiled and nodded, looking from the paper back to her, watching as she retreated slowly down the path. I would definitely do as she asked. I may not know how or why, but this woman had given me a literal second chance at life, and I was determined not to waste it, because I had a feeling that I was also getting a second chance at love. Not too bad for my first day back from the dead; getting a gorgeous woman to kiss the life back into me and managing to get her phone number almost simultaneously. I glanced down at the paper again and bit my lip. Then I smiled. I was sure I would see Carolina again... if only I could figure out how to work a phone.

AUTHOR BIOGRAPHY

Jelaina Jones grew up a voracious reader and lover of all things fantasy. She believes that magic is real and is still bummed she never received her Hogwarts letter. When not reading, attending book clubs at her favorite local bookstore, or rearranging her bookshelves, she's writing, cooking, or working as a Navy civilian. What she does for the Navy, no one quite knows, as she would have to kill anyone who found out, (not really). She shares her Central Pennsylvania home with her two crazy cat familiars, one hyperactive dog and one gamer boyfriend. Her first novel, a second chance sports romance, is tentatively set to be published summer 2021.

16

Back Cover Artist's Note

Judy Kelly

Once Upon A Magical Day With Poppy, Rose, And Cat...

One of my favorite parts about creating my art is gathering ephemera. I love artifacts that have history and tell a story. My favorite places to wander for these vintage treasures is at flea markets. I get lost in a time capsule and its history when I am looking at all of the ephemera that surrounds me. My mind goes whirling with all the ideas of how I will create with each piece I collect. I have to admit that the hardest part for me is each time I shuffle through vintage photos. I just wish their families could have them. But when I create with them I feel like I upcycle and give them a new story!

In this piece, "Once Upon A Magical Day With Poppy, Rose, And Cat..." I left their story open ended so the viewer could tell their own story. I used a vintage cigar box for the stage and an old cardboard jewelry box for the platform which I collaged with vintage papers. Poppy and Rose were vintage paper dolls. I collaged their dresses with dictionary, music, chemistry, and crossword puzzle vintage papers. The ticket was from the Carousel Ride at Knoebels. Cat was cut out of an old children's math book and topped with a fairy hat to be festive like Poppy and Rose. So, What do you think Poppy, Rose, and Cat did on their magical day together?

To learn more about Judy Kelly's art please contact her at skipbay@comcast.net

Judy Kelly

BACK COVER ARTIST BIOGRAPHY

Judy Kelly, Back Cover Artist
Piece: Once Upon A Magical Day With Poppy, Rose, And Cat...

This is my journey... I want to be brave...

I have always been a person that is shy and quiet. I am a great listener but inside I am just bursting at the seams to share my story! It took me a long time to create my art for me. I was always trying to create what I thought others would like and enjoy. But I knew something was missing.

One day long into creating I realized that if I created my art for me then it was sharing my story and who I am as an artist. All of a sudden, my creations came alive and I was so much more fulfilled! Now, all of my art creations tell my story and are a little piece of me. I believe it is never too late to try something new, follow your dreams, believe in yourself and just be you!

Share your story... I became brave...

ABOUT STORY MAKERS

Story Makers is a twelve-month long writing class run by the Cupboard Maker Books, featuring one class a month with a different instructor each month. 2020 was the inaugural year of the class. The goal is to introduce writers at all stages of their writing careers to new ideas and techniques for not just writing but also navigating the publishing world. The authors in this anthology range from never-been-published to multi-published.

The 2020 instructors were: Misty Simon; Geri Krotow; Carrie Jacobs; Briana Michaels; Kristian Beverly; Samantha Coons; Heather Heyford; Natalie J. Damschroder; Bill Peschel; Teresa Peschel; Maria V. Snyder; LuAnn Billett; Laurie J. Edwards; and Michelle Haring.

To learn more about Story Makers, visit cupboardmaker.com/events/storymakers

CPSIA information can be obtained
at www.ICGtesting.com
Printed in the USA
BVHW091314240621
609509BV00002B/5

9 781733 183741